The Toymaker

JD BALLAM

velluminous

Published by Velluminous Press
www.velluminous.com

ISBN: 978-1-905605-15-6

Book Design
Holly Ollivander

The Toymaker

For
Lydia, Alistair and Clarissa,
who love toys.

Chapter One

A single note—high, firm and unwavering—rests on the humid August air.

At last the voice of the singer fades slowly into a smile that is satisfied with the look of the surrounding fields, deserted and fragrant with newly-cut hay. Above the young man's right shoulder, the fields rise gradually, ending in an upward turn of scrub that is lost in the steam-shrouded oak woods. The crops, mostly corn and hay, tattle in the occasional breeze. On his left hand, the earth rises sharply—or rather the old gravel road has crushed its way into the soft hillside—and above it he can just see the outline of further green-gold fields, tipping upwards into the distant haze-crested mountains. There is no sound but the butting of grasshoppers in the tall grass by the ditch, and the dragging lisp of locusts in the trees. Under the boiling indigo skies the birds are silent, there is little movement and nothing lowers its shadow on him except the early-withering leaves of the walnut trees. He pauses only

once on his journey, pushing aside a mask of vine leaves that
hides heavy bunches of wild grapes hanging uncollected by
the roadside.

As he looks down at his feet he notices for the first time that
his new walking boots are powdered blue with the strange
dust that carpets the road. He looks backwards and is disappointed not to see a long trail of this dust following him down
the slow descent to the village below. Evidently, the grotesque
humidity, unlike anything he has ever known, quickly presses down what elsewhere might have been his tracks in the air.
This same humidity had filtered its way through his mouth,
leaving behind a staleness like old butter, before passing in a
stricturing way through his lungs, and ending up in wide wet
circles under his arms. Hours before, he had given up taking
any notice of the flames that tingled up the small of his back,
trapped beneath the fresh weight of his backpack. Twelve
miles ago he put this pack on for the first time as he stepped
down from the only bus that came anywhere near his destination. After a fourteen-hour flight he had been in America for
less than a day. He had ridden from the airport to a medium-
sized town, got some vague directions, and then started walking. On the way, he had passed through only one single-road
village, and now, at his feet, was another even smaller one.
But unlike the last one, this one had shade and a crossroads.

Almost without warning, the road twisted away. Two hard
bends snaked in opposite directions, and afterwards the road
flattened into four mis-aligned turnings. On the hillside above
the crossroads were two houses. The larger, built from a kind
of moss-green stone that he had seen nowhere else before
today, stood well-back from the road at the centre of a large
farm. The other, shaped exactly like the first—and like every
other house he had seen in the district—was a long two-story
rectangle with verandas on both floors. Although all of the
shutters were open—a fact which he thought strange—the

dark interiors looked as cool as pond-water. Immediately in front of him was a small shed painted sage green, and diagonally opposite it, a tall brown barn full of farming equipment. Two more farmhouses, one red and one white, were visible in the distance. But what caught his eye was the building opposite the shed. It seemed to be a house, but he saw no sign and no parking, just a closed screen door and a cherry red Coca Cola machine under the little porch roof. On the left hand side, nearest him, was a rusty steel chair, and in it an old man sat dozing.

This was the first local that Matteo had seen, and he eyed the sleeping man closely as he approached. The old-timer wore grey trousers, white socks and enormous brown lace-up boots. He had on a boiled-white shirt, open to the navel, and black suspenders. With the man's head lolled to one side and largely hidden by a black-banded white straw hat, Matteo could see nothing of his features except a silver and black stubbled neck, and a dense tangle of hair that covered chest and shoulders alike. Cautiously, Matteo stooped to get a glimpse of the man's face — and jumped back when he saw that the shaded green-grey eyes were wide open and staring at him.

"I'm sorry."

"How do?"

"Hello."

"You thought I was asleep, didn't ya? Well, I been watching ya coming down that hill for a hell of a while. I ain't never seen nobody walk as slow as you. You alright, boy?"

Matteo gazed uncomprehendingly for a moment. Although his own English was faultless, this man's words were not like any he had ever heard. Besides, this was no way to talk to strangers.

"Is this a shop?"

"Yes, sir, it sure is. You look like ya need a drink."

Both men glanced at the Coca Cola machine, pulsing in the shade. The old man waited a moment, but Matteo, having no change and feeling too awkward to ask for any, didn't move. Finally, his host stood up and rattled a knobbly blue-veined fist into his trousers.

"Well, sir, the Good Lord was mighty pleased when the Samaritan gave that feller some help, and I reckon I could do the same." He stuck out a hand. "Ephraim."

Matteo accepted the offered handshake, and smiled. "Pleased to meet you. I'm Matteo."

Ephraim quickly dropped two coins into the machine, opened a long skinny glass door and pulled out two green bottles of Coke. He grinned waggishly at Matteo. "It's cheating to pull out two, but then it's my machine." He popped off the lids and handed Matteo a bottle. "Here. I ain't never seen nobody a-looking so thirsty as you."

Matteo nodded and took a long pull at the cold drink. The old man looked at him. "Where ya going?"

Matteo stopped drinking and held the cold bottle to his temple. Squinting in the sun, he considered his answer. "To a place near Scravel."

"Scravel?" Ephraim's high voice screeched even higher. "Well, I'll be damned. You sure come a long way to go nowheres."

"What do you mean?"

"Ain't no place near Scravel."

Each took another swallow of Coke. The old man looked at his visitor, sweating in the sun. "You got friends there? Cause it ain't much to see. Come on down here and I'll show ya the way."

Ephraim stepped out into the sun and waggled side to side down the hill, and Matteo followed him to the perfumed shade of the maple trees knotted around the crossroads. The valley was a minor one, running perpendicular to the main shelf between the mountains and cut through by a wide rock-strewn stream that he had neither heard nor seen before. He looked along its banks to the right, near the houses, to where clouds of midges twirled in the shade between lime-green patches of sun. The stream itself was shallow, and the bed peopled with beige stones the size of men's heads. The tumbling water was clear as glass where it leapt into the air, but as dark as coffee against the stones.

Matteo was struck by the fact that the bridge he walked over was only about two feet above the water. "Why is this bridge built so low?" he asked.

There was a silence, and he realised now that the old man had been speaking non-stop for the last five minutes, and that he had heard nothing. They both grinned.

"Well, we used to have them up high, but for some reason the floods used to knock them right off. So, we started to put them real low, and now if the water gets high, it just washes right over them." Ephraim paused. "You still want to go to Scravel?"

Matthew nodded. "Yes … sir." He seemed to be catching the old man's politeness. "More than anything."

Ephraim's smile faded a little, and he got on with his directions. In the midst of turn right here, and past this or that farm and Old Man So-and-So's place, he hesitated, looking hard at the brand new boots and backpack that Matteo had bought for the journey. "You sure this ain't some kind of mix-up?" he demanded. "You sure you ain't got the wrong Scravel?"

"I'm sure."

Ephraim nodded doubtfully and picked up his direction-giving where he'd left off. "Now ya got all that?"

"I think so."

"Well, if ya don't mind my asking…" Ephraim laid his hand on the long wooden axe handle that was strapped to Matteo's pack, and gave it a shake. "What ya planning to do over there?"

"I'm looking for an old house."

"Gonna knock it down?"

"No. I'm going to move in."

Ephraim laughed. "Shit. What ya going to live on, trees? Cause there ain't nothing else except rocks."

Matteo clenched his jaw. "I'll be all right. I was born around here."

Ephraim stopped laughing so suddenly, he looked as though he were going to be sick. "You was born where?"

"In a house up a long dirt track, with pine trees on both sides of the road, and a pile of white stones on the corner. There was a tree with white flowers, and another one with pink ones. There was a spring that made the little field soft in places, and rabbits in the rocks of the wall. The house was painted blue."

Ephraim considered for a moment. "I know this mountain good as anyone. There's only one blue house near Scravel. Ain't nobody lived there for years. Must be twenty years or more. Feller that lived there…" He paused and Matteo waited, dry-mouthed. "Feller that lived there up and got his self shot. Then his woman run off. Back to her people, folks reckon. Now what was his name…?"

Ephraim trailed off, looking expectantly at Matteo, who had the impression that the old man knew the names of everyone between the Potomac River and the Mason-Dixon Line, and that he was being tested. He remained silent.

"Durrent," Ephraim said at last, staring off into the distance. "That's it. George Durrent. His people was from Bethel and his mammy used to take peas down to Feageyville, to the train, every spring. Then she died and left him that old place." His eyes turned down from the sky and he looked Matteo straight in the face. "What in the shit you want to do up in them bushes 'round that old place?"

Matteo, who had never heard his surname pronounced

quite like this, stared at the ground. "I've come to look for something."

"What? Ticks and skeeters? Cause you sure going to find plenty."

"No." Matteo looked squarely at Ephraim. "Memories." He didn't like to think of his mother being described by the likes of this man as somebody's 'woman.'

"Whose?"

"My mother's. And my father's. George was my father." As he said his surname, pronouncing it in the way he had heard it almost all his life, he gauged Ephraim's reaction. The old man stood absolutely still, the crookedness of his back making him seem shorter than before.

"Je-sus. Then you're George's boy! Well son-of-a-bitch." He suddenly drew nearer and the sweat on his face glistened. "Hey, ya ain't looking for no...trouble, are ya? Cause folks don't know nothing about what went on up there all them years ago."

Matteo—with a forced show of joviality—put his hand on Ephraim's shoulder. "I'm not looking for revenge. My mother's told me the story. I'm just ... I'm just looking for my ... myself. My first childhood."

"Your what?"

But Matteo didn't answer. He let his hand fall, smiled, and walked away.

"Hey!" Ephraim shouted. "Your name's Matthew, ain't it?"

Matteo stopped. "It is."

"Well, Matthew, ya want to bring me that bottle back here so as I can get my two cents for it?"

About an hour later, after Matteo had taken Ephraim's advice and followed the road to the right as it wound its way alongside the stream and into the forest, he came to a junction just as the old man had described. The main road wandered to the left, around a stony meadow, dotted with briars and flanked by a family of oak trees—all of whom appeared to be children of the enormous parent that stood in their centre. Two more farms were in sight now as the level ground began to widen, but both looked smaller, probably because of the poorer soil. The front of one of the barns was decorated with three white circles, each sprinkled with red, yellow, blue and green shapes in a pattern that Matteo found oddly reminiscent of something.

On the right, crossing the stream he had been tracing since he last saw another human being, stood a tall narrow iron bridge, painted leaf green. It was obviously very old and it rose up on tall ramps absurdly high over the water, but beside it there was a sign saying 'Crow Rock.' Ephraim had said that this was the shortest path to the house that Matteo was looking for, so he turned and made his way upwards into the cooling darkness of the dense woods.

He went on, glad that most of the long late afternoon sunshine was burning its mark on the leaves thirty feet over his head. Sometimes he went for more than a mile without feeling the sun at all. The air was partitioned into silent rooms of scent—pine, honeysuckle and the rose-rich balm of multiflora— and Matteo's heart swelled with dreaming.

All at once he stood still. There in front of him was the corner that Ephraim had described. A long narrow brown shed, open at both ends and shaded on the west side by a half-sunken-in tree aching with tiny worthless green apples. Matteo's breath left him. Twenty feet further on, before yet another uphill shift in the road, was a small embankment where the setting sun came into view, making the air luminous with the reflection from a mass of white stones hedged all about with purple phlox. He had found his first memory.

Forgetting the weight of his back pack and the miles in his legs, Matteo ran down the dark lane that he had sought in his imagination for many years. The way was rutted by rain, and cross-scored by fallen branches, but he tumbled on until he reached a shaggy, sapling-sprouted clearing. The house — utterly unlike anything he could remember — stood dirty and disused on a wide, terrace-like plot of land on the mountain's south-west face. Strangely, Matteo felt his arms lighten, and he dropped his pack near a sawn-off tree. Like all the houses he had seen, this one was a long two-story rectangle, with a wide porch on either side, running the entire length of the building. Inquisitive and never uncritical, he also saw that no windows appeared to be broken — even the white curtains all hung in place. The roof seemed sound, the electricity line still ran up to the building and — despite being wild and overgrown — the land near the house was not as bad as he had feared.

Then he had a disturbing thought. Suppose Ephraim was mistaken about the house being deserted? Several of the houses he'd passed — tiny tar-papered shacks — looked far worse than this. Perhaps someone had moved in.

He walked cautiously to the rear of the house. Everything his eyes lit upon jangled in his head, spoiling his concentration and provoking minute scenes and flashes from long ago. In the far corner of the porch hung a black iron swing that faced away from onlookers, preferring to turn its occupants towards the vast panorama of mountains and fields below. Urns and pots lay everywhere, packed with rotted vegetation that had grown up, re-seeded, and died in cycle for season after season. A hand-plaited rag rug that he recalled some old woman showing his mother how to weave, was still in its place, like a pile of humus on the floor. To the right of the doorway stood a tall metal cylinder with a head like a mushroom that he remembered had been known as 'the milk can,' although he never knew the reason why. He went over to the door and tried the latch. It was locked. Whether by instinct or something else he didn't know, he put his hand on the milk can and tipped it backwards, rolling it along to one side. A centipede, a spider and a caravan of wood-lice scuttled to safety, and he saw the front door key, wet and brown, in the centre of the rusty ring left by the can—possibly in the exact place his mother had left it.

Trembling, he picked up the key and—with difficulty—slotted it into the old lock. It was the first time in his life he himself had unlocked the door. After a moment of stubbornness, the mechanism gave way, and he lifted the drooping door up slightly on its hinges and let it sag downwards into the room.

The simultaneous strangeness and familiarity of what he saw cleared his mind of everything else. The door opened into the kitchen, where everything was as neat as if it had recently been tidied. The cupboard doors were all closed, with no visible marks of damage by weather or animals. The table still stood where he remembered it, with the chairs all neatly pushed in. There was a lumpy white fridge and a huge white enamel sink. The walls—formerly white—had faded to a deep cream, the same colour as the linoleum that undulated with the contours of the floor. One end of the room was completely taken up by a huge wood-fired range whose bare-iron surfaces were skimmed with corrosion, and with the tawny dust that hung in drifts over everything.

The parlour, too, was almost unchanged, with its crowded black-cherry furniture and its deep blue curtains, now faded into an exact copy of the folds that they had held for two decades. The space he remembered his father calling 'the room'—meaning the sitting room—smelt fusty and damp; Matteo passed through quickly to climb the bare wooden stairs up to what had been, for five years, his own room. But he hesitated when he saw his parents' open door. Their tiny room was dominated by an enormous brass bed, the mattress of which was waist high. Around the edges were two chests of drawers and a washstand, all built of oak and all with marble tops. A strange chill pinched the nerves in Matteo's neck as he glanced at the bathroom with its cast-iron tub, and his ears whirled with the sounds of his mother's laughter, her face pink and dappled with soapsuds.

He went quickly through the third bedroom, the one that had been nobody's, and into his own little room. His bed still crouched beside the window above the porch, and he remembered lying there on summer evenings like this when he had been forced to go to bed while it was still light. He remembered, on those evenings, looking out over the tremendous valley that cast itself away from the mountainside where he was born, and waiting for the cool night air to waken the songs of the mockingbirds.

Like all of the cupboards in the house, apart from the kitchen, his chest of drawers was still full. Inside it he found little shirts in colours and plaids he had forgotten, most of them scarcely wide enough to wrap around his arm. The table where he had once drawn a great workshop for his father was untouched, the drawer still full of papers and pencils. Nothing in this room—or in the entire house—was damaged or broken or unsettled. Everything remained exactly as he and his mother had left it, and the very perfection of its emptiness pushed through his throat and beat at his eyes. He sat down on the bed and slowly wept.

He woke up with a shudder. Realising exhaustion had got the better of him, he called himself stupid. He tried to think of what he had to do. The room, the house and the huge strangeness outside was a sheet of utter darkness, patterned only by star-light. He forced himself to stand, though his knees wobbled and his calves vibrated. Now that his sweat had cooled he realised for the first time that he smelt unwashed. His stomach felt like an empty bottle and his head seemed not completely under his own control. He remembered that he had left his pack outside somewhere. How was he to find it in the dark? Moving cautiously, he made his way downstairs into the kitchen. He was surprised that he remembered the way, and yet the distances all seemed wrong. He had left the kitchen door open, and cursed himself for doing so. It must have been the first time for years, and such things made him angry with himself.

He crossed on to the porch and ran straight into the dislocated milk can. Gritting his teeth in renewed anger at himself, he replaced it and then picked his way back towards the lane, relieved that the starlight was bright enough to guide him to his bag. The trouble was that this action ended the entire sequence of his plans; he was hungry, but working out how or where to eat seemed impossible. His pack seemed even heavier than before; for Matteo, manhandling it down the slope to the porch became a sort of penance that helped him forgive himself his earlier transgressions.

He crossed the porch and sat on the swing. Opening out before him was the vast and all but featureless landscape of the valley, as silent and fragrant as an empty church. In two or three places he could just see the yellow-white lights of houses, and from the farthest reaches of the mountain he heard dogs barking. But near him there were no sounds except the jittering of the swing's rusty chains and the beating of his own heart.

The pressure of the backpack against his arm reminded him of the hollowness in his stomach, and he groped with dust-caked fingers at the unfamiliar zips. He was a stranger to this sort of equipment, and although he had planned his packing style for more than a month before setting out, he could not remember in which of the little side pouches he had stowed his evening meal. After a great deal of rustling, he pulled out half of a round loaf, unbuttered; a small uncut salami; a jar of olives; and an orange. Too weary and too bewildered to search for his all-purpose camping knife, he bit off a hunk of bread and chewed distractedly. How strange to break out of one space and into another. He fished in the jar for an olive, spat out the pit—and then cursed himself: this was not the way to behave on the mountain.

From what his mother had said, it might be the only olive pit for fifty miles in any direction. As Matteo smiled to himself, he saw that splinters of white light were falling through the trees as the moon rose above the mountain-top. Now that he had the opportunity to examine his hands, he was horrified at their dirtiness. Without thinking, he drew the bottle of mineral water from his pack and used most of it to wash them, realising too late that his only other drink was an unopened bottle of wine meant for his first special occasion. Baffled by this uncharacteristic surge of mental incompetence, he set the backpack down at his feet and began to rummage for the wine. There, wrapped in socks, he found it. Even in the shimmering silver light its pinkness touched his heart and called him back to tenderness and the realities he knew.

The wine was special to no one but himself, and it was special to him because of who had made it. It was pink because Nonno couldn't make it any other way; for three-quarters of a century it had given its colour to Nonno's cheeks. Matteo had lived with his grandfather for twenty years, drinking this wine freely at the old man's table, confident that every year was a special vintage. It was only in the last few months, since Nonno died, that Matteo came to understand that the few bottles which remained to him must be drunk with respect for the love that had engendered them.

He set the bottle down carefully, punishing himself with a mouthful of dry bread. What, after all, was he doing here? He had answered the question a thousand times in his head, preparing explanations for anybody who might ask, including himself. He had even worked out rebuttals for the doubts he knew would beset him when he arrived. Yet the moonlight and the strangeness of his feelings still lay in tight circles around his neck and shoulders, binding him to the question. Was he lonely? Glancing at the wine, he answered, yes. He'd had every good reason to forget these wild forested hills.

After his mother took him away, he had struggled to loosen himself from this world, replacing it with the verities of school, church and friends. To everyone who knew him, Matteo's childhood was unexceptional. He was strong and — being the offspring of an Italian mother and an American father — he could speak English better than his classmates, an ability that granted him the distinctiveness which all boys crave, and that propelled him to study French and German as well. His passion for study narrowed and deepened with the arrival of his teen years, and his mind wrestled to prevent any further loss of the memories he now knew had enriched it. He had spent precious hours of night-time and vacations dreaming himself back into the places and among the people he had known. This particular joy had raised him in his mother's estimation, and he treasured her all the more for holding two worlds in her eyes. He would see them there often when she sat, ill, broken, and ghastly with the disfigurement left when a great love has been ended by death. It was this spirit that rocked within her on those long summer evenings, stirred only by church bells and by the sound of his voice reading. When she died, he kept the memories as her legacy.

The contours of early manhood he owed to his grandparents.

Nonna—a large ferocious blend of sweat, perfume, goodwill and commotion—made no effort to take over her daughter's role. Matteo honoured her wisdom for this. Instead, she alternately beat him and baked him sweets, listened wide-eyed to his friends' tales of his university prize-taking, and swore among her cronies that he was sure to have a secret love somewhere, knowing that by doing so she pawned the truth in favour of her dearest wish. Her death left Matteo and Nonno almost destitute, with nothing left to spur them in the way that only a woman's love can; nothing to lend ardour, risk or satisfaction to the things that make up daily living.

He never quarrelled with Nonno. What either one wanted, the other agreed to. They discussed all the things that men discuss over coffee, and parted each day liking each other. They were proud and they were true to one another in the way that the best families are. So when Nonno died, Matteo cried only once. Resting his lips against the old man's empty forehead, he said a short prayer of thanks, not for himself only, but for all that Nonno had made of life.

And so with a little of the money that had been left to him, that had been wisely invested and re-invested in the ways that keep money returning, Matteo took some time off from his own life to examine his past.

What he found lay about him in unrelated heaps—maps with pages that didn't join, rooms with windows and no doors, stars that illuminated no one but themselves. So he set out to chart his own mind, bringing with him the things that gave his memories substance. He reached into the bag and drew out a pair of joined wooden wheels, painted red, with yellow and blue diamonds—a child's Ferris Wheel toy. He had known it almost since his world's first focus, and it—like the others he drew from the bag—had been all his father's handiwork. There were cars, an aeroplane, an abacus, two spinning tops. Lying on its side in the starlight was a jaunty, worn marionette, its face turned towards the forest, where its smiling eyes rested unseeing. There were more than a dozen hand-made, hand-painted extravagances that a poor man had made for his only child. Matteo touched them one by one, glossing them with his fingertips. Fool that he knew himself to be, he had truly brought the barest essentials for his trip.

After a time he lay back in the swing and cast his fortune in the orange peel. He couldn't deny the rashness of what he had done, but he was satisfied, at least, that the combination of derision, fascination and slight panic suffered by the only local person he had met was exactly what he had calculated it would be. Nothing remained now but to restore the house, and to prepare himself for eventualities.

Listening to the night-breeze lower its wing over the uppermost leaves, he began for the hundredth time to mark out a trail for himself. As he did so, the cold purr-whit of the mockingbird lifted up from the branches behind him, and his plans darkened into sleep.

Chapter Two

News of 'Matthew's' arrival rolled up and down the mountainside as quietly and surely as the morning mist. Although everyone in the vicinity held a pretty good picture in mind of what he looked like—and some even interrupted their chores to stroll along the lane that led to his house, just to catch a glimpse of him—he had been seen out and about only once. On that occasion he had walked to Ephraim's shop and asked to use the telephone. Ephraim duly reported that Matthew had taken a piece of paper from his pocket and telephoned a taxi. He then disappeared; the taxi collected him near the low-water bridge about half an hour later. No one saw him return, so he probably did so after dark. This too impressed the locals.

The next day was Sunday and it dawned with ripe summer blueness. Inside Matteo's house, a domestic miracle had been worked. Every sign of dust, mould, disuse and disrepair had been removed. He had worked practically non-stop in daylight and in dusk to clear away webs from the corners, rust from the hinges, and stains from the walls. He left nothing untouched that water carried from the stream, heated over a fire and mixed with a combination of travel-wash and shampoo, could clean. Although his mother had scrupulously removed all traces of food from the house before she fled, he still found an excuse to blame her for two old corn brooms left imprudently bristle-side down, and bent into near-uselessness by the weight of two decades.

Aching, dry-skinned and bemused at not having accomplished even more in the past two gruelling days, Matteo went out into the clean morning air. Apart from the business of his single outing, he had seen very little sunshine since he arrived and — as there was nothing more to do indoors at present — he decided to take a walk. He shouldered his time-softened leather haversack and threaded his way through the cluttered porch, picking up his axe and laying it across his shoulders like a yoke, with a hand on either side, just as Nonno had taught him as a boy. Matteo still carried the axe this way, whenever he walked in the woods. He was tired, but his mind felt freshened, both by the work he had done and for the return of an old habit.

A little further on, Matteo came to the path he had already worn into the undergrowth by his trips to and from the stream. The path was not really his own, as it was plain that the trees on either side had been cut back at some time, leaving a widened channel of light in the leaves. Countless varieties of birds, whose songs he didn't know, pirruped in the still-damp air, and sometimes dropped, pert with curiosity on to the stones that had been cleared away to either side of the path. He looked down at them, admiring their propped-back stance that neither welcomed nor rebuffed him, but simply considered his presence with healthy curiosity. When he reached the pool of the stream where he had lowered his bucket for water, he looked around attentively for the first time, taking in the contours of the ground. On the opposite bank, he saw a narrow muddy patch, dark with little tracks where evidently something came at night to drink. The brush behind this patch was noticeably thinner, so he decided to follow the animal's example, and see what he could find in the woods beyond.

Never without a purpose, Matteo pushed on, telling himself that he should familiarise himself with the boundaries of his land—and he made every effort to keep his mind on his task. But against his wishes, the power of the forest exerted itself. Yellow-mint ferns as wide as fountains laughed against his trouser legs as he brushed by them, and drifts of dead leaves, never before shaken by footsteps, plunged under his strides. He paused to grip and shake the bark of a hickory tree, to test its firmness, and once he stooped to cup a fiery red feather in his hands. More things gradually pushed their way into his senses and he began to delight in the strangeness of the sounds and smells. He found a pile of acorns shorn of their caps; a pyramid of earth, kicked up by some burrowing animal where it had dug parallel doors to its home; a greasy black tree shimmering with thorns; a cedar branch, sinister in its opiate richness. The crackle and smack of water over stones drew him on ever quicker. He had already grown to love these streams—though they were low, barren-looking and untidy—believing that in them he had found the source of something in himself.

Sitting on a boulder, he caught sight of a large greenish-brown globe, lurking lazily in the sunshine where the trees bordered a small clearing. This triggered a memory, and Matteo couldn't resist the impulse to stalk the immobile vegetative target, crouching low and walking with exaggerated secretiveness. Twenty feet from his quarry, he waved the axe over his head, broke into a run, then did a terrific hop on to the giant puff-ball fungus, which erupted into a dense, filthy cloud of spore. Matteo was still grinning with satisfaction when the silence of the woods was rattled by the flurry of a chainsaw.

The sound came from the hillside opposite, and Matteo could see now that he had climbed a small ridge, beyond which lay a wide grassy weed-and-rock strewn meadow that after another downward turn, merged with the forest again. As much as the recent solitude had comforted him, Matteo felt compelled to investigate, and set out across the meadow. Pulled back to his usual preoccupations, he cursed himself for having made so little progress in the boundary investigation; he must make up for this laxness by meeting the neighbours.

When he reached the far edge of the clearing, he saw that he had been mistaken about the resumption of the forest: what he found was a wooded fringe, with more open land beyond. Some of these new fields were cultivated, bordered by strips of rocks and trees so that they seemed sewn together like the old quilt on his bed. The buzzing whine of the chainsaw came from the corner of a corn field, a little distance from where Matteo now stood. As he skirted this plantation he paused to admire the crop, which was flourishing despite the stony soil.

Once clear of the tall corn, he paused to observe the wood-cutter. The man was dressed in a bright orange shirt and fad-ed jeans. He seemed to be working alone, bent over his chain-saw at the base of a medium-sized fallen tree. At first, Matteo thought the man had botched his task, dropping the tree onto the wire fence between two fields. But as he got nearer, he heard the woodcutter quietly swearing, his muttered curses blending with the slow *put-put* idle of the chainsaw. Finally, he turned the machine off and, laying his hands on his hips, roared out obscenities in an inverse proportion to the stillness he had re-created.

Matteo could see the problem plainly: the saw was irrevocably wedged into the tree. The collapsing timber had pinched itself together on the chainsaw's bar, making the job impossible.

Matteo waited for a pause in his neighbour's shouting, and discreetly scuffed his feet on the ground. The man spun around, drawing his heavy, sun-bleached eyebrows together and clearly prepared for an argument. The first thing that struck Matteo was that he had never seen a head so like an upside-down turnip—wide, with curly root-hairs on top.

For a moment, the two of them stared at one another. Matteo was about to speak when the man's demeanour changed, and he gave a broad, crooked smile. "Howdy! Don't mind me, it being Sunday and all. I didn't hear ya come up. I don't usually do no work on a Sunday, but this here tree's fallen over and broke the fence down, and I got to fix her up before the cows gets out."

Matteo extended his hand. "Hello. I'm Matteo Durrante."

"Yeah, I thought ya must be. My name is Jonas Farley. Pleased to meet ya!"

He took Matteo's hand with a grip that was as strong as his language. "Well, and how ya doing up there?" He eyed Matteo's axe. "Getting them bushes and trees cut up?"

"No, I haven't started yet."

Jonas's eyebrows found one another again, but they parted quickly. "Well, sir, you come along just in time, cause I sure as hell got this god-damn saw of mine stuck." He patted the tree trunk, and rolled his small eyes around to Matteo. There was no malice in them, nor embarrassment, only the twinkle of merriment and a bit of joshing.

Matteo stayed where he was, studying the tree. Whatever happened in the next ten minutes was sure to form this man's opinion of him, possibly forever. It would also make its way into the gossip of the nearby hills. For better or for worse, the problem had only two possible solutions. The tree had fallen across the angle of two fences, leaving the trunk jutting upwards so that the saw was suspended about three feet above the ground. It might be just about possible chop upwards toward the saw, relying on the tree's weight to snap the weakening timber, but only if he could swing the axe in such a cramped space, and if he cared to spend most of the day at the task, and if he could make himself forget how decidedly unmanly such mincing little blows would look.

The other possibility was to cut a wedge downwards towards the blade, freeing it from the top. This would take both a good aim and persistence.

Without speaking, Matteo laid the axe down, slipped out of his haversack, and dragged a flat stone off the nearest fence-row, positioning it near the tree where its height would raise him up enough to bring his full strength to bear. As Jonas looked on in silence, Matteo picked up the axe, stepped on to the stone, and set to.

Chips flew rhythmically, easily, with a crack and hum. As Matteo's cut deepened, the wood deformed downward under its own weight, re-filling the gap almost as quickly as he made it. Nevertheless, it wasn't long before for the smooth, narrow wedge had chopped nearly through to the trapped bar and chain.

Matteo laid the axe aside and pushed a sweat-soaked strand of hair from his eyes. Without looking up, he grasped the chainsaw and pulled its starting rope. He had never used a power saw like this before, but he judged that as this one was still warm, it would probably start. He was right. Bucking and spurting, coughing out chips that smelt of rain, incense and oil, the saw wormed its way out of the tree. Matteo turned it off quickly and placed it on the ground, well away from the timber. With the blind single-mindedness that work always gave him, he still said nothing, but instead seized his axe and leapt up on the heavily-gouged trunk. He rained down three blows with his head facing Jonas, then three more from the opposite direction. He then looped the axe handle behind his head as if he were once again out for a walk, spun around, and bounced heavily in place. The tree made a twanging noise, followed by the sound of a thousand threads scissoring as it collapsed into two separate hulks. Matteo jumped clear, landing flat-footed on the stone.

Having completely forgotten that he was helping someone else, Matteo remembered too late not to look over-pleased with his success. He glanced around, relieved not to find Jonas where he expected him to be, but also a bit disappointed to see him sitting in the dappled shade of a young tree, busy with a short tin cylinder.

Matteo went towards him, recognising now that the cylinder was some kind of lunch pail. "I think it's alright now. I didn't see any damage to the saw." It was hard not to feel a bit surprised at Jonas's lack of interest.

Then Jonas looked up at him, and Matteo saw a tremendous face-squashing smile spread across his face.

"Alright?" Jonas said, "It sure as shit's alright. I'll be damned if I seen anybody swing an axe like you since I was a boy. Ain't nobody even uses an axe no more." He shook his head in thrilled disbelief. "Son-of-a-bitch, that was something."

Matteo stood dumbly for a moment, unsure how to go on. Jonas, too, was pretty plainly agitated by the whole thing. "Now, you don't need to be going yet. You ought to sit down here in the shade for a minute and eat a little something." He prodded about in his tin cylinder, peering inside as if he wished he had more to offer. Finally, he tilted his head to one side, and grinned waggishly. "Say, bet ya ain't never tasted Lebanon baloney have ya?"

Matteo hesitated, not at all sure what he had been asked.

Jonas took this as his cue. "Go on then, sit yourself down here and try some."

Matteo, a little blown in the chest and sore in the arms glanced upwards at the razor-sharp light of the mounting sun, and made up his mind to accept Jonas's offer. He retrieved his haversack from the grass and weeds, and returned to sit in the shade opposite his neighbour. Jonas reached into the pail and removed a lump of something wrapped in greasy brown paper. He then unclipped a huge knife that he wore in a leather scabbard on his belt, and used it to cut off a piece of whatever it was that had been wrapped in the paper. He handed the portion to Matteo, winking at him with anticipation.

Matteo accepted the offering: a half-moon of purple-brown salami, as wide as his palm. It was warm and slippery and the pepper and salt it exuded mingled with the smell of sawdust on his hands. He took a bite, and the sweet taste of cured fat and meat-cooked-to-hardness seemed to welcome him even more than friendly words. He felt himself relax as he chewed.

"That's Lebanon baloney." Jonas said, nodding his head.

"It's good. Very good. Did you make it?"

Jonas laughed in his stunted way. "I'm tickled you might think so, but that's too fancy for me to make. Esther's daddy makes it." He stuck his hand into the tin again and pulled out a chequered cloth. "Esther's my wife. Hey, I got some bread here she baked yesterday. You want some?"

Matteo considered Jonas as the other man studied the cloth for a moment and then unwrapped its contents. How childish and uncomfortable Jonas seemed, awkward and stumbling in a way that Matteo hadn't expected to find in his neighbours. What touched him most was Jonas's apparent hope that Matteo should like him.

Happier with himself, Matteo took the lead, pulling his haversack onto his lap. "I have some food too," he said.

Jonas, studiously unwrapping the quarter-loaf, gave no sign of having heard. Their hands met as each offered the other a portion of the lunch they had brought. Laughing, Matteo took the bread, and gave Jonas a short orange-tinted salami. Nervousness spread itself over Jonas's face as he looked at the exchange.

"It's salami. I brought it from Italy. It's very good. I think you will like it."

Jonas smiled like someone about to swim a deep river, and put a little into his mouth. As he chewed, the scents of garlic, fennel and chilli swept around both men, into their eyes and up their nostrils.

"Well, sir, now that's something. I ain't never tasted nothing like that." Jonas sighed contentedly and slipped a second morsel between his teeth.

For some time, the two of them sat chewing in silence, occasionally swapping a bit more salami, or cheese. Matteo even went so far as to persuade Jonas to try an olive — a thing which was altogether new to him, and which he evidently didn't like. Looking down at the candle-flames of light that fell on them through the tree, Matteo thought it was at last time to ask a few questions.

"Is this your farm?"

Jonas swallowed hard. He seemed awfully pleased to be asked a question. "Yes, sir, it sure is. Been mine since Ma died, and she got it after Daddy died, and I reckon his people had it since way back when. Yeah, it ain't much but it's all I need. I got some cows and chickens and I don't know what-all running 'round here. And I got some trees of all sorts, you know, apples and peaches and pears … and plums and cherries. It ain't real big but it's enough for me to do till my boy grows up, and that ain't going to be for a while yet, cause, well, he's still little. I don't grow much hay cause the fields has got too many goddamn stones in them, and they break up the mower blades.

No, it's all I want. Gets cold as hell in the winter, but then there ain't so much to do then. I just sit around and get fat. Yep, I ain't never lived nowheres else, an I ain't a-going to."

He finished this speech, and lay back looking so content that Matteo thought he was going to fall asleep. One eyebrow then slid up a little higher than the other one and he squinted to ask, "How about you?"

"I've been cleaning up the house for two days. I just wanted to see the sunshine a little." Matteo looked out over the surrounding fields from where the burring thrum of insects was beginning to rise, though the weight of the day's growing warmth still pressed hard upon the drying grass.

Jonas closed his eyes. "Yeah, it'll be hot for another month, probably. You by yourself, then?"

"Yes, I am."

Jonas said nothing for a moment. Matteo wondered what the other man was thinking. "I've still got a lot to do outside," he said at last.

Jonas opened his eyes and raised himself on to one elbow. "You going to do it all yourself, are ya? I'd sure like to help ya, but I got a powerful lot just to keep up with my own. Yes, sir, I'd like to help. Now, there might be somebody who could give ya a hand —"

Matteo interrupted. "No thanks, I won't need any help."

Jonas looked surprised. "You sure? I'd like to, but like I said ... well, I don't know how I'm a-going to get it all done as it is. I mean," and he looked around conspiratorially, "every day ain't a Sunday."

Matteo took this as a hint, and pulled himself to his feet. "No, it isn't, and I've still got a long way to go." He looked around the hillsides, reassuring himself about the fiction of the boundary examination.

"Where ya going?"

"I thought I'd see the boundaries."

"Going to have a look at your fences, huh? That's a good idea. Good fences makes good neighbours is what they say." Jonas hauled himself up. "Hell, I can least show ya 'round your fences, being Sunday and all."

Matteo frowned. "What about your cows and the broken fence?"

"Well, they're in the field on the other side of the barn. I shut them in, and they'll be alright for a while. They ain't a-coming this way till milking time. Come on then."

Before Matteo could answer, Jonas was on his feet and six paces ahead of him. "Let's see that axe of yours," he said, turning.

Matteo passed the tool over and watched Jonas examining it, not without expertise. The blade was silky smooth, free of nicks and without any signs of file or forge, even though it was a hundred years old. The handle, though, had one small dent in the blade side, and Jonas laid his fingertip on this and rolled his eyes towards Matteo.

"You miss too, once in a while, huh?"

Matteo considered the question. The dent was almost as old as the axe itself. Nonno had said that his father—the greatest woodsman in the family— had missed a blow, once, when his mind strayed to thoughts of a woman. 'And this,' Nonno had said with his finger raised, 'is a lesson to all men who work.'

"It was my grandfather's," Matteo said at last.

Jonas nodded, and handed it back as they reached the first fence. Once they had both crossed to the other side, Jonas became a different man. Matteo watched as he shunted along in front, his heavy feet swinging as they bore the burden of his rocking side to side. As soon as it was possible to do so, Jonas plunged his hands into his pockets, from which they seemed irretrievable. He also seemed compelled to raise his head and squint in whatever direction sunlight was available through the thickening leaf-cover. As they reached another corner where four fences met, Jonas stopped and leaned backwards, looking out over his chest in the way birds do, at a stone-edged enclosure that sloped downhill somewhat, and where the trees were noticeably smaller than those in the surrounding fields.

"This here field's yours, and so is them two down there on the right." He gave a melancholy sigh. "Yeah, this one used to grow real nice taters when I was a boy, but it sure ain't worth much like this."

Matteo climbed up on the ridge of stones that acted as a foundation for the posts along which some rusty wire was strung, and laid his hand on a tree that was nearly ten inches across.

"What kind of tree is this? I don't recognise them and they seem to be everywhere."

"That's a locust tree," Jonas said. "They grow pretty fast."

"What's the wood like?"

"Well, it's real good for fence-posts and all, cause it don't rot. I reckon these is locust." As he said this, he shook hard at the top of one of the posts beside Matteo, proving that the wood was still sound after more than twenty years. "Your daddy probably put these up."

Matteo flinched. Jonas looked away and quickly changed the subject. "Ya even got some sulphur in here," he said, digging his boot toe into the stones and scuffing up a tropical-coloured yellow dust. "You can dig it out and give it to your cats if they get distemper."

Jonas trailed off into silence, as though he had given too much advice.

Matteo climbed down from the stones and set off again. "Are there many chestnut trees around here?"

Jonas followed, quickly taking the lead again. "No, ain't no chestnuts. They all died years ago. Mostly oak, poplar, sycamore, hickory…and like you done seen, locust. Even the ole elm trees is a-dying."

"What's the matter with them?"

"Aw, I don't know. Something foreign. Something foreign to come in and…" He stopped, and turned around to look at Matteo. He was standing with his chin far downwards, smiling faintly. "Aw, I don't know. Things is always a changing. I expect it'll all be alright. If it is, it is, and if it ain't, it ain't. Ain't even worth a damn to burn."

"What isn't?"

"Elm."

Matteo nodded. They had now reached the summit of a low rise from where much of Matteo's land could be seen. The three fields that Jonas had pointed out lay beneath them, running up the side of the mountain where they could take in the afternoon light. As Matteo looked down on them — now little more than straggling unkempt forests, the timber from which could fence his whole farm twice over — his mind reached easily into its pocket, drawing out a single late-summer day from his boyhood when he had carried water from the house to his father, who worked down there alone. Now, nothing stirred except the noise of starlings, and the clamour of a nest of robins ejecting a blue-jay from its midst.

Behind him, across the deep groove in the hillside shaved out by centuries of running water, he could see his house among the trees. Turning, he could also just see part of the view that was visible from his front porch, and he realised how much care had been taken in siting the house.

Jonas, who had been watching as these ideas passed like clouds across Matteo's face, now came over to him. "'Course everything between here and the house is yours, including the crick. There's a spring up behind the house, stuck in the hill there." He pointed over Matteo's left shoulder. "Them woods is yours all the way up to the Dance Hall Road where it meets the ole reunion grounds." Turning, Jonas pointed beyond the house. "And that field down there full of trees is yours too. Your neighbours on this side, they all got cows, like me, so the fences is pretty good. 'Round there though, ain't nobody done nothing since Daddy died twenty years ago."

Jonas had slowed down over this last sentence, and Matteo thought it worth asking more, just in case he owed Jonas a favour on his family's account. "Did your father do much work on our place?"

Jonas stepped away, and rammed his hands even deeper in his pockets. "No, no, not too much, just this and that. He was a real nice feller and all, did what he could. No, not too much." He laughed a little nervously, and went on a few more steps. "Hey!" He stopped and pointed at a growing plume of dust. "There's somebody coming down your road."

Matteo stood beside of him and watched as a huge yellow-sided truck made its way along his rutted lane. Without speaking, Matteo swung the axe up over his shoulders again and passed down the slope towards the stream and his home. Jonas still stood in the same spot.

"So, why don't you come too?" Matteo shouted. "I'll give you a hand with your fence later."

For a moment Jonas hesitated. "Ain't no need for…" Then he shrugged, as if surprised at his own change of mind. "Alright then, if you want to."

When the two men rounded the corner of the house, the truck was parked and a man in a green uniform had just knocked loudly on the door for a second time. He had the angry look of a driver whose directions have been poor; who has found the roads unexpectedly bad and the lane to the house appalling; and no one home at the end of it. Matteo hurried over to him. "Hello," he said.

The man turned with puckered lips and released a great "Ah…" that seemed laden with significance. Without another word, he motioned towards the truck, where the passenger-side door opened and a second uniformed man sprang down. The first man looked at Matteo. "Are you Mr Doo-ranty?"

No longer surprised at how his name could be pronounced, Matteo nodded.

The man smiled. "Any relation to Jimmy?"

The joke was entirely lost on Matteo. Conceding defeat, the driver continued, "We've got your delivery all inside. In eleven years I ain't ever had a delivery this big, or this far, and on a Sunday to boot. Where ya want us to put it all?"

"Put the tools over there under that tree, and everything else here on the porch."

"Will do." He turned towards the second man. "C'mon, Bill, lets get the heavy ones down first."

In a moment, Bill and the driver were hard at work unloading the truck, all the while repeating the singular story that never in eleven years had so much stuff been taken so far on a Sunday.

Forgetting that he was standing in the direct sun, which now leaned its sinister crest upon him, Jonas looked on with his forehead wrinkled low over his eyes. What he saw astonished him. This was evidently an independent transport firm that, judging from the address on the side of the truck, his new neighbour had hired in Baltimore to deliver a range of goods.

These purchases passed by in front of him—Bill, it seemed, specialised in carrying the lighter items, which he placed under the tree where he had been directed. There was a bowsaw, a hatchet, splitting wedges, a steel mallet, leather gloves and apron, two handsaws, a mitre saw, planes, punches, hammers, awls—an entire workshop's worth of hand-tools. All this was unloaded while he watched the other man wheeling large and small boxes onto the porch, which Matteo painstakingly cleared for him, stacking up even the rubbish with unusual care.

When the work was finished and signed for, Jonas—red-faced and sweating, though he had lifted nothing—crossed over to the porch while Matteo carried boxes one by one inside, stacking them meticulously in the kitchen. Unwilling to come on to the porch, he waited until Matteo looked up at him.

"Ya want to get them tools in tonight before the dew gets them."

Matteo set down the box he was carrying and wiped his forehead on his sleeve.

"I'll dry them all and oil them before bedtime."

Jonas's eyes widened. "All of them?"

"Of course. They are new and it must be done properly." Matteo picked up the box again and carried it into the kitchen.

Struck with wonder, Jonas shouted to Matteo, "Hey! Give me a rag and some oil and I'll get them going for ya."

By nightfall, the most important things were all put away and Jonas's broken fence was repaired. Walking back up the hillside alone in the darkness, Matteo took a moment to reflect. He was not tired, but without electricity, there was little that he could do by candlelight.

He entered the house and closed the kitchen door behind him, then took down the matches and candles from the shelf where he had laid them in preparation for this evening. In their dim reposed light, he sat down for the first time since his impromptu lunch under the trees. His eyes rested on the packing cases of food, hauled from seventy miles away at such expense. He had planned this purchase carefully; if he were frugal, the tins of vegetables should last until spring-time, when he would begin to grow his own food. Simple per-ishables he could buy locally, while other special items would be delivered in the coming days and weeks. As for house-keeping: Matteo's stock of kitchen utensils, supplemented by a few recent additions, was now adequate to his needs, as was the linen supply.

The new washing machine might require a plumber, and Matteo blamed himself for neglecting to ask Jonas if he could recommend one. Indeed, he had also forgotten to ask about the spring, which might need a new pump. He was sure there had been running water in the house when he was a boy, but the finer details of pumps and piping escaped him. Perhaps Jonas knew.

He laughed aloud as he imagined Jonas's possible replies. In the twelve hours of their acquaintance, Matteo had seen anger, timidity, conviviality, admiration, pride and bashful-ness roll their heavy wheels across his neighbour's wide face. As the two men went side-by-side under a gold-edged night sky, hurrying to dismember the fallen tree, Matteo listened to Jonas telling about two decades of his life. He spoke of hours upon hours of unrelenting anxiety, watching the green of his crops deepen as storm-clouds drew darkly above the moun-tains. He rubbed his neck hard when he told of the blinding tide of work that came with the spring.

And yet, how soft, even feminine seemed the heart of the man when he spoke of his wife, his daughter and his son. In the shadows that masked them, Matteo could see the joy that lay like a silver flower in Jonas's eye, when he told of his 'good, too good for me, Esther', 'that girl of mine' and 'my boy.' Jonas plainly worked hard for his living, and even harder against the mundane sadness of isolation, and this work gave him peace—a peace that Matteo longed to call his own.

Chapter Three

"Yes, sir, I like him. He come along and stood in there and done the work of two men without nobody asking him, and what's more he did it real good. Shit, I don't know when I last seen anything like it. Not for years. Well, that axe looked like a part of his arm. Then he come 'round in the evening and worked till sundown—now he didn't have to do nothing like that, did he? And it was hot as hell too! No, sir, he's alright and I like him."

Two children crouched in the shadow of a stand of sumac trees, each one striving to be more quiet and attentive than the other. These words of their father's—spoken only two days before—bounced around in their heads and made curious questions swell up hard around their Adam's apples as they waited.

While they listened, Jonas had told the men who gathered at Ephraim's shop in the evenings how he had met the stranger and how they had worked side-by-side on the fallen tree. Desperate for anything new in the waning days of their summer holiday, the children had, over a period of forty-eight hours, been laying plans for how they might get a closer look at Matteo. Finally, they put on the only green clothes they had (for camouflage) and crept off in the clinging half-light of the morning to hide themselves in the bushes and see if the man himself would appear.

They were not disappointed. While they both were beating on each other's shoulders to enforce a silence that neither one would have dreamt of breaking anyway, the back door of the house swung open and Matteo came out. In his left hand he carried the fabled axe, and both children stared until their eyes began to dry out.

In a moment, without looking around, Matteo strode into the medium-sized tangle of brushwood with the confidence of someone who had played there as a boy, and stretched his arms wide. He pulled and contorted this way and that, bending at the hips, pulling and loosening at the muscles in his arms and legs, until he was ready. Then, without the least reflection, he began to swing the axe purposefully, knocking away at the spindly trunks that had grown up into a chest-high forest.

The children looked on in wonder. They had seen axes used before—to cut off small branches, to chop firewood, to split old timber—but never had they seen anyone clearing a patch of ground with no more than an axe. And so the *tip-pink, tip-pink* of the blade was fascinating, for a while.

Yet after about ten minutes, when Matteo had swiped away at an area about eight-foot across, the need to see more got the better of the younger child. Despite his sister's pulling at his arm and shirt-tails, he crawled forward and crouched behind the deep-brown gravy-fumed stump of a long dead tree, to get a better view. Matteo stood up a little straighter, but did not turn around. The sky had ambered over sumptuously and a rich dew-laden breeze tingled upon the leaves, and he raised his eyes to look out over the steadily lightening valley before him. A woodpecker *clippocked* noisily against a branchless dead tree and a whirl of crop-scents was carried upward from the farms below.

Matteo began to sing.

For the children, the magic was complete. Never, except on the radio, mutteringly in church, or garishly from the stage at the annual fire department carnival, had they heard a man sing. This was something too wonderful to be believed. Amid the tearing sounds of the saplings, there rose up a soft voice that sometimes swelled with pride, and sometimes seemed on the verge of tears.

It was some time before either child realised that they couldn't understand a single word of it. Certain that the answer lay in listening harder, the little boy slid around the tree stump and crept forward until he was just behind the place where Matteo had begun to pile up the broken trees and branches. Ignoring his sister's wild gesticulations, he stood up to get a better view over the heaped tree limbs, pressing the topmost branches down to clear his field of vision. As he did so, the hastily-made pile collapsed with a loud *shoosh*, and Matteo turned around. Two pairs of eyes met, but neither person spoke.

Matteo was so surprised that he couldn't think of what to say. Here was a little boy—maybe six years old, maybe eight—wearing jeans and a green baseball cap. His green flannel shirt—much too small and obviously saved from a winter or two before—had its tails out, and although it just managed to reach his trousers, it was certainly a strange thing to wear on what surely would be another hot summer day.

"Hello, neighbour," he managed at last.

The boy hesitated, with the wide-eyed mortification of a child who has caught a grown man singing. "Well, hi."

"Are you out hunting?"

"No, sir."

"Oh. Have you lost something?"

"No, sir."

"Do you need any help?"

"No, sir. I was just wondering what that song was you was a-singing."

"Sully!" a little girl's voice scolded from somewhere.

Matteo looked up, and there on a tree stump was another child, a girl of perhaps ten or twelve, and she too was dressed oddly. She wore a green dress that looked like it might once have been her Sunday best, and green socks with work-shoes. She jumped down and strode sternly towards the boy.

"Ya oughtn't to be asking folks questions like that, prying in to other people's business," she told him. She looked up to Matteo, and smiled in a very grown-up fashion. "Hi."

Matteo nodded and looked at the boy, apparently named Sully, who stood there expectantly, obviously hoping for an answer.

"Is this young lady your wife?" Matteo asked him.

"No! We ain't married. She's my sister."

"Oh. Would you like to introduce us?"

The boy was well and truly stuck, but the girl stepped up and put out her hand. "My name's Ruth Ann. How do ya do?"

Charmed, Matteo shook her hand and made a low bow. "How do you do. I am Matteo Durante."

Ruth Ann stepped back bashfully, and Matteo looked again at the boy, who remained resolutely silent.

"And your name is…?"

Ruth Ann spoke up. "Sully!"

"No it ain't!" the boy answered crossly.

"Yes it is."

"No it *ain't*!" He put out his hand to Matteo. "My name's Marcus."

"Sully!" Ruth Ann teased.

Ignoring her, Matteo gave the boy a good manly handshake. "Hello, Marcus. I'm glad to meet you."

"Matthew, know why I call him 'Sully'?" she pressed on, stepping in closer.

"Shut *up*!" Marcus snapped.

"Cause when he was born, Mama showed him to old Mrs Warrenfeltz—who used to be a schoolteacher— and she said, 'What's his name?' and Mama said, 'Marcus, cause that's Roman,' and Mrs Warrenfeltz she said, 'That's a good idea calling him something Roman, cause he sure gonna sully his self plenty.'"

Marcus, infuriated, pushed her hard against the shoulder, but she laughed him off. One step ahead of them, Matteo, looking seriously at the boy, held the axe handle out towards him.

"So, Marcus. I wonder if you could give me a hand? Could you carry this up there to the corner of the porch for me? I want to move these things, and then I'd like a drink."

Marcus smiled and then took the heavy tool and bore it proudly to the porch, shooting a defiant, triumphant look at his sister as he did so.

A few minutes later, the three of them sat with their backs pressed to the front wall of the house, their feet dug into the leaves and pointing downhill. Each held an enamel cup. The children watched eagerly as Matteo uncorked a bottle of wine—the first either had ever seen, and one of Matteo's many new store-cupboard items. He poured a small amount into each of their cups, and watched in amusement as the children looked with greed and scintillation at the dark rose-coloured fluid they had been given unasked. Unable to think of a suitable English phrase, Matteo raised his cup to the sunshine, and beckoned. "Salute!"

He took a short slow eyes-up drink and watched Ruth Ann and Marcus tentatively tasting theirs. The sky overhead had warmed now to a deep hyacinth blue, and the tattering sound of the leaves had slowed as the heat of the day weighed upon the breeze. Both children, happily wandering in a faeryland where anything could happen, were so completely absorbed that Matteo was reluctant to break the spell. At last he laid his hand on Marcus's shoulder, and the boy looked up, licking the purple ring off his lips.

"So, Marcus. Where should I start to work next?"

Marcus looked around, giving real consideration to the question. Jealously, Ruth Ann spoke up. "I think ya ought to start right here."

Marcus disagreed. "No, he ought to go back to where he was before. That'd make the most sense."

"Aw, what do you know? You're just saying cause you want to be different from me."

Matteo got to his feet. "Marcus, I'm surprised at you. Don't you know we must always do as ladies ask? Ruth Ann says we must work here, so we will work here."

"But—"

"And you, Marcus, shall choose the tree."

Satisfied, Marcus looked around and pointed at last to a tangled dogwood tree near the corner of the house. "There. That one blocks the light to the windows. Do that one next."

Impressed by the boy's practicality, Matteo nodded and went to the spot indicated. He hadn't realised that the view over the valley deepened from this corner, taking in more of the lower hillside—including the field where he had helped

Jonas with the fallen tree. He followed the lane with his eyes until it disappeared into the woods, where he could just make out the outline of a red house and barn.

The tree Marcus had chosen was taller than many of the others, and branched out widely at shoulder-height. Lower down, it showed signs of having been pruned in the past, but long years of neglect had allowed suckers and summer-growth to clutter up its limbs. Matteo chose the smaller of its two main limbs, just above a fungus-packed Y, as his target, and with four blows lopped off a sizeable part of the tree. Before Matteo could speak, Marcus was on his feet and dragging the severed portion away. Then using his axe like a plane, Matteo sheared off many of the littlest branches, which — not to be outdone — Ruth Ann painstakingly collected.

The children's helpfulness was not without its drawbacks, as Matteo had to be doubly careful not to swing the axe when either was near. And as they had now begun to compete openly, the timing of his work became increasingly problematic.

"You know, this is a flowering tree," he said. "It would be a shame to fell it completely."

"Seems like it'll die anyways, from that fungus," Ruth Ann said.

"Well, let's see what can be done to tidy it up." Matteo chopped down hard, just above the place where the fungus had invaded. The blade wedged in the thickened wood, and as Matteo levered it free, he was surprised to find a streak of rust on the axe's blade. Kneeling to examine the cause, he grasped the loosened base of the shorn limb and prised it off.

As it came away, he saw a stretched and crumbling rectangle of metal, buried inside the tree and still spotted with white enamel. It was pretty plainly a little ferrous box of some kind that had been hidden or lost in the fork between the two limbs when the tree was much younger and which had, with the passing of time, been enfolded completely by the wood.

Unaware of anyone else now, Matteo picked at the surface of the box, and the side nearest him bent and gave way. Looking at it closely, he saw that it was some kind of package, marked with a faint picture of a bearded man.

Suddenly, his mind drew him back to an afternoon with his mother, playing a game of chase around the trees near the house. After catching her for the fourth consecutive time, Matteo had demanded a ransom before 'letting' her go. All she had was a song, she said; would that do? Matteo agreed, and the song she sang haunted him with its beauty; he still remembered how his arms had weakened to the sound of her voice.

When she'd finished, he asked her to teach him the song, and she said she could not, but she would write it down for him. Later, he took the paper and put it in a little box, hiding it under the tree where she had sung it. Now he looked again at that little box, and there inside he saw some darkened shreds of paper. He took these out and read:

Solo e pensoso i piu deserti campi
Vo mesurando a passi tardi e lenti,
E gli occhi porto per fuggire intenti
...
Perche negli atti d'allegrezza spenti
...
Si ch'io mi credo omai che monti...
E fiumi e selve sappian...
Sia la mia vita, ch'e celata altrui.

In Matteo's ears, the leaf-struck air carried his mother's voice once again.

Meanwhile, Marcus and Ruth Ann had grown impatient. As far as they could see, the little scraps of paper were useless, and being completely familiar with hiding things in trees, they saw this as nothing special.

Marcus pulled at Matteo's elbow. "We going to cut some more?"

Matteo smiled at the boy, stuffed the song into his pocket, and picked up the axe. Thinking quickly, he strode away from the children, selected a tree at random, and toppled it. Almost before his young helpers could begin clearing up, Matteo had bounded to another part of the hillside, choosing and felling trees as widely separated as possible. In this way, he provided the children—and himself—with more than enough safe work.

In time, the palm-wide leaves of the poplars, swaying on the perpetual breeze, formed and re-formed little triangles of light that exploded like fireworks on the stony ground. The furrowing *hinch* of tree limbs, so like the whispering of wave tops over their heads, came to be the only sound as the birds—exhausted by the heated air—sat mutely above them.

Alerted to his progress by the sting of hunger, Matteo slowed down to look around him. In only a little while, he had struck down a forest of saplings, portions of which silvered the carpet of leaves that slanted up to his house. Marcus and Ruth Ann, loyal to their ambitions but much more slowly than before, still dragged broken bits of wood on to the piles that now towered above them. Matteo's heart knocked with affection and real gratitude as he watched his neighbours toiling amidst the debris.

"Marcus," he called out, "we must stop, or there will be nothing left for the birds to hide in. And you, Ruth Ann... a lady who works so hard deserves a fine lunch."

The children looked at one another. "Let's stay," Marcus said.

Ruth Ann gazed longingly at the house, but said, "Well, I

expect we ought to be getting on home, cause we ain't told nobody where we was going. Ain't that right, Sully?"

Marcus's lips compressed and he looked at his feet. "Aw, it don't make no difference."

"You don't want Daddy coming up here after us, do ya?"

The boy's shoulders sagged in defeat, and he turned silently and headed home. Ruth Ann looked at Matteo, smiled with absolute politeness and said, "Bye." Then she too, set off downhill as enigmatically as she had arrived.

Matteo was caught off-guard by the suddenness of their leaving. He shouldered his axe and followed them.

"Wait a moment," he said. "You mustn't go until I have thanked you." The children turned towards him. Matteo thought quickly. "I know, I'll give a present to your parents. Where do you live?"

"Down there." Marcus pointed to Jonas's house.

Matteo waved his hands in surprise. "Then you wait here. I will be right back."

He disappeared back up the hill and returned in a flash carrying another bottle—but unlike the first, this one was filled with pink wine, and it had no label.

He gave it to Marcus to carry. "With this we will celebrate our new friendship."

Going down the hill to Jonas's house took more than twice as long as it ought to have done. This was because every few minutes, or every few steps, the children stopped to show Matteo something they thought he ought to know about. They pointed to the dim grey arcs of the turkey buzzards leaning lazily against the depth of blue sky. They pried open the wires of a fence to show him the spot where the dead skunk had rotted for months because it had smelt so bad that no carrion-eating animal would touch it. Together, their hands held the smooth yellow funnels of the honeysuckle, pinching off the bases and pulling out the long stamens to touch against their tongues for the drop of 'honey' they contained. They whistled at starlings, plucked the seeds off fox-tails and threw stones at the high green knots of walnuts still in the trees. By the time they reached the wide tree-shaded circle of Jonas's farm, their friendship had been made.

Beyond the rutted stone-packed lane that led to the barn and other outbuildings was a white picket fence that marked off the farmhouse's dooryard. Inside, Matteo felt instantly the fondness of familiar things: orange and white geraniums butted against one another in heavy clay pots wherever there was sun; climbing roses rocked nonchalantly against the deep red brick walls; paths lined with white stones twisted crookedly from doorways and concealed doorways, showing the directions taken by each day's work; and over all a verdant darkness that kissed the skin tenderly and coolly after the harsher glint of the fields. He followed the children's footsteps as they scuttled around the corner of the house towards a door that pointed in the direction of the farmyard. Once again, he saw the flame of light against the walls and green shutters, and heard voices as the screened door banged shut after them.

"Land-sakes, what are you young ones a-wearing? And where you all been?" a woman's voice called.

"Matthew's come with us! Matthew's come along with us!" Marcus answered. "He's come for lunch and he's brought some wine too, and we had some, and it's real good, and now he's got some for you and Daddy."

Matteo followed the children to the screened door. Inside, the woman who had called out was drying her hands on her apron and looking worriedly at her visitor. Matteo bowed slightly, and wiped his mouth nervously against the back of his hand.

"Well, don't just stand there Marcus, open the door," she said.

The boy did as he was told, and Matteo stepped inside. The woman smiled at once, albeit weakly, and stepped a bit closer.

Matteo took the lead and extended his hand. "I am Matteo Durrante. How do you do?"

The woman's fingers, red and hot from recent work, slipped away from his own. She rubbed her hand uncomfortably against her temple. "These two brats of mine been bothering you this morning, then?"

"No, no. They have been helping me to cut down some of the little trees and undergrowth that surround my house. They have worked very hard, and I've come to say thanks to you, and so say thanks to them."

Matteo looked away from his neighbour, who was obviously not used to being spoken to by strangers, let alone men, in her own kitchen. She seemed to be in her late twenties, and her face, like her hands, was pinked with the heat of the day and by the work she had been doing. Her hair, long, deep brown and almost straight, was pulled away from her face and tied with a ribbon at the base of her neck, but little strands that had been scorched white by the sun clung to the sweat on her forehead. When she smiled, and her smiles came and went very rapidly, Matteo thought that she had a fine profile—the only view of her face that her discomfort permitted him.

Marcus pulled at his mother's elbow. "He wants lunch."

She looked up quickly, and Matteo, seeing her green-grey eyes for the first time, wondered if she were afraid.

"Mahh-UM" Marcus droned.

"Yes, yes, I done heard ya the first time, boy! Go and get your daddy in here and tell him his lunch is ready." Marcus started off, and she called after him, "And wash them filthy hands of yours."

Ruth Ann, who had already washed her hands, took a seat on the bench that separated a large wooden table from the window at the far end of the room. As she did so, the lumping sound of Marcus's feet died away on the stairs, and Jonas himself appeared in the doorway near the table.

"Well, sir, and how are ya?" Jonas bounded happily across the room and gripped Matteo by the shoulder.

Relieved to see his friend at last, Matteo began to relax. "I've been working on those little trees around the front of my house and Marcus and Ruth Ann have been helping me. I didn't know who they were, or I would have brought them home a little sooner. They must have plenty to do here."

"Je-sus! You got them two to do some work? Well, I'll be damn." He ran his hands through his sweaty hair, pushing it up in little curls. "No, sir, you put them to work. You put them to work. That's good for them." He went over to the sink, where his wife had just finished washing the dishes and was now drying them. "You hear that, Esther? He done got some work out of them. Damn if he don't know a thing or two."

Embarrassed, Matteo stared down at the pink and white linoleum on the floor, studying the way it rose and sank in waves over the floorboards underneath. His eyes followed the trail of wet footprints, left by Jonas's sweaty feet on the way to the sink. Jonas was now bent over, washing his hands and still chuckling over the notion of his children working voluntarily.

Marcus appeared through the same doorway, and brought a towel to his father before sitting beside Ruth Ann on the bench.

Jonas turned, and his wide-cheeked smile dropped away as he looked at his wife. "Well, come on then, Esther. Ain't ya never had a guest for lunch before?"

Esther gave her husband a worried look that seemed to suggest she never *had* had a guest to lunch before, and then smiled briefly and wiped her hand against her temple. "Maybe Matthew'd like to sit beside of you, huh?"

Jonas beamed, and waved his hand towards the table. "Sure!"

Matteo slid onto the bench beside Ruth Ann. Feeling the bottle still in his hand, he remembered its purpose. "Here," he said to Esther, "I have brought you this as a thank-you for your children's help, and to say ... well, to say I am pleased to be your neighbour, and that I hope we will all be friends."

Esther took the gift, peering at its neck as if she had never seen such a bottle before—and it suddenly occurred to Matteo that quite possibly, she never had.

Jonas stepped in. "Here, see if we got a opener in the drawer."

Esther stood up, looking about the room as if she were quite certain that the required opener was in one of the kitchen drawers, if only she could recall which it was.

Before she had taken two steps, Matteo spoke. "I have one here that I carry on my knife when I work outside."

He took the knife from his pocket, unfolded the corkscrew and began spiralling the metal tool through the soft wood of the cork. As he pulled, the cork left the bottle with a gentle *ponk*.

Esther took down three tumblers from a cupboard and brought them back to the table. The children looked more than a little disappointed, but evidently preferred not to press their luck. Matteo poured out three glasses of Nonno's wine, tiny drops running over his fingers and falling silently onto the table.

As the meal evolved into a cluster of family conversations going on happily without him, Matteo took the time to look around the room.

It was a cream-coloured, high-ceilinged space—at least twice as high as most men were tall. The walls were crowded with wooden store cupboards, squeezed so tight against the ceiling that a ladder would have been needed to reach the upper shelves. The sink, where all the washing had taken place, was a zinc-lined cupboard, above which two bright nickel taps projected from the wall. Apart from an over-sized (and certainly recently-acquired) refrigerator, the kitchen held no electrical appliances except for the huge stove. The centre of the room was empty, and large enough for at least three more tables such as the one around which Matteo and his hosts now sat. The room was lit by four large windows, at this hour mostly in shade, and by a long shaft of light that came through the open doorway to his left—the one through which Jonas had entered, and which was now behind Esther's back.

He looked at Jonas's wife. Why had she not introduced herself? Now that Matteo had faded into the background, she was utterly at ease with her family as they discussed the state of the corn in the 'high' field, the probable cause of Mr Murphy's girl's absence from church, and the likelihood that Tippy's fleas would get transferred to Marcus's bed. Her thin cotton dress, back-lit now by the sun, revealed that her upper arms were slender, not bulked out by constant hard work. Her eyes twinkled with pride at her daughter's mock coquetry, and it was only when she met Matteo's glance that she looked down and self-consciously brushed at an invisible stain on the apron she still wore.

When the fried chicken, sweet corn, mashed potatoes and gravy had all gone, and been followed by wide wedges of cherry pie, the children vanished quietly and quickly. Matteo had not expected this, but he said nothing, instead re-filling his hosts' glasses with the wine he had brought, thinking that sooner or later, after a little banter, everyone would return to their chores.

Rosy-cheeked, Esther turned to him and asked, "So what

was that paper that Marcus said you found in that tree and went all funny over?"

Both the unexpectedness and directness of her question threw him off balance, and he chided himself for not having noticed the boy's comment the first time it had come around. "Oh, it's nothing," he said. "The words of a song that my mother wrote down for me when I was a boy. I hid them in the tree then, and I found them today."

Without really meaning to do so, Matteo took the scraps of paper out of his pocket. Esther smiled and gazed at him, and he suddenly understood where Ruth Ann had learned to cast her eyes about in the way she did.

"Well then," Esther said, "if there ain't nothing to them, I suppose I can see them?"

"Esther!" Jonas exclaimed. "Maybe it's private."

Matteo shook his head and handed Esther the scraps of writing. "No, there is nothing in them that is personal, except that they are in Italian."

Esther looked at them as though they were charms, and said nothing. Jonas cleared his throat and drained his glass. After a moment, Esther looked up at Matteo with a friendliness that was utterly new, a warmth that he would not have believed possible, a moment before.

"She must have been something, your mama. She was from them places, wasn't she?"

Matteo looked away. "Yes, she was."

Jonas took up the thread of the conversation. "Yep, that's right. When George was drafted he went straight over there to Italy, but he didn't come back till two years after the war was over. Never did learn what them fellers did all that time there, after the fighting was done, but when he come home, he brought her with him. Don't know what she saw in this old place, but she sure took to it right away. Yes, sir, I remember she was a happy woman, always a-smiling. I remember her real well, cause I was a boy and I saw her 'round a lot, you know. Yeah, she liked kids, alright. Then after you was born, I didn't see her so much. But I heard folks say she was real nice, and all."

Esther, whose eyes were wider now then ever, gave the scraps back to Matteo, and looked at him mischievously. "She sure must have loved your daddy to come all that way to live here."

"She did." It was Matteo's turn to look hard into the spaces over their heads. "When I was a boy, I remember Papa used to sit in a rocking chair by the window, in the evenings, and Mama used to sit on the floor between his knees, with her chin on his leg, and they laughed, and they tried to teach each other songs, but he could hardly sing, and her hair—it was still black, then— used to hang half over her face and stick in her mouth. Nonno—that's my grandfather—told me that during the war, that if we were not poor, we were not rich, and anyway, when they met it was easy to see which way things were going to go. Nonna tried her best to talk Mama out of him anyway, but Nonno knew it wouldn't work, and that even if she was his only child, it was better to be in love really, even if that meant she would go away. And who knew, if it was bad, they could come back, there would always be communists for the Americans to fight."

Matteo realised that his was the only voice raised in laughter, and stopped. Esther was gazing at him as if entranced, her wineglass held untasted at her lips.

"Yes," he said more quietly, "they were more in love than anybody."

Jonas, his glass now empty, slid back his chair and got up. He rubbed his close-set eyebrows. "Well, sir—Matthew—that sure is something. I like to talk about old times, I mean folks is folks, ain't they?" He laughed.

Matteo took the hint and stood up too. "I didn't mean to

invite myself to lunch. Really I didn't. I just wanted to say thank you. And the children…well…" He rolled his eyes to the ceiling.

"No, that's alright, ain't it, Esther? You come round anytime you want to. Shit, we're always home." He pulled his shoes on without tying them. "Here, you come on with me. I got something to show ya."

Matteo nodded to Esther, hoping she'd take it as a hasty thank-you

"No, now, don't ya worry about a thing," Jonas said. "Esther'll take care of the dishes." He practically pushed Matteo out the door.

Jonas seemed to relax a little once he got outside, but he still set off at what was, for him, a rapid pace. When they got to the farmyard fence, he stopped and propped himself, with one leg drawn up a bit, against the boards. Curious to hear what would follow, Matteo did likewise. The sun drew little wet beads on Jonas lip as he began to talk, while Matteo looked out over the deserted farmyard, hard-baked with dung.

"No, its alright," Jonas said. "Well, ya just got to know that Esther…she's a little, I don't know…special about some things, I guess. She'd do any damn thing for me, I know that. She just gets all funny talking about, well, folks and love and all. It's alright, ya know, I mean I love her like…well…"

He shook his head and stared at the ground. "Its just she's a little soft like about it, you know. I mean she likes talking about it, like a woman. I mean, your folks was special and I guess she's heard all about that, and now she wants it from the horse's mouth. Shit, ya get her started an she'll have you down here every damn day, talking about them times." He inspected his hands for a moment, then squinted up at Matteo. "Say, your mama ever say much to you about what went on then? About why she left here and all?"

Matteo spoke slowly. "She left because someone shot my

father. She needed money to live. And besides," he said, glancing towards the house where Esther was at the window, washing up again, "the love had gone out of her life."

Matteo turned back to Jonas, whose face had become tight and strained. The moment was cut short by the sound of Marcus, coming towards them from around the far corner of the barn.

Jonas pointed to a tree behind the boy's shoulder where a pair of weather-beaten corn-dollies danced from a limb. "You know anything about pear trees? Cause every year that goddamn tree gets covered with flowers, then don't have nothing but little bitty pears that ain't no damn good at all."

Chapter Four

As Marcus and Ruth Ann knelt among the pole beans, slowly harvesting the dry rattling pods that held next year's seeds, a delicately-pitched sound reached down to them on the simmering air from above the canopy of sere yellow leaves, burnt-edged by the sun. They turned their eyes to the hillside where the blue glint of Matteo's house could be seen half-hidden by late-summer leaves.

They listened, and once more there came the gentle rocking of his voice as it swung happily through another melody that they had never heard. Without saying anything, without even looking at one another, the children dusted down their scratched palms and went slowly towards the lane that led to his house.

Listening and looking about them, they tracked Matteo via a circuitous path, following the sound of his voice as he moved through the woods. They finally found him kneeling by a damp deep green circle of grass just above the stream, where their father's cows sometimes came to feed. He was wearing a straw hat of a type that neither had ever seen before, and there was a wide flattened basket by his side. They thought at first that it might be an Easter basket, except that it wasn't Easter, and anyway, the eggs would have rolled out of the sides. Peering at him from their hiding place in a scrub-oak coppice, they were astonished to see him pulling up large tufts of a clover-like grass and laying them delicately in the basket, next to several other varieties of greenery.

Unable to contain himself any longer, Marcus stood up and went towards him. "What ya doing, Matthew?"

Matteo looked up, stuffed a few leaves in his mouth, and smiled. "Picking grass to eat for my supper."

Matteo watched the boy's face for a long moment and determined to say nothing else until Marcus said something.

After a minute, Marcus pursed up at him in the sunlight. "Won't ya get sick?"

"No. It's not really grass. Come here."

Marcus went closer. Ruth Ann jumped out from the coppice, the swampy ground squelching under her shoes as she ran to them.

"Here." Matteo gave them each a frail and broken little stalk with a few leaves on it. "Try some." Neither child moved to accept, so he continued, "It's called watercress. It grows wild here. My mother showed me this spot when I was a boy; I used to pick it for her."

Ruth Ann tentatively reached forward, pulled off a single leaf and put it in on her tongue. Not to be outdone, Marcus then took a good-sized pinch and stuffed it into his mouth, crunching through the stems.

"Tonight I will have a salad, and tomorrow night I will have soup," Matteo said, kneeling down again and pulling up a few handfuls more. The children crouched by the basket and poked at its contents with their fingers.

"What else ya got in here?" Ruth Ann asked.

"Them's dandelions," Marcus answered, picking up a long leaf and holding it up to the light. "I know what that is."

"Yeah, Mama cooks them sometimes. But what's that old grass stuff?" she asked, pointing to some long, carefully-stacked tubular blades.

"That's wild garlic, Daddy says. He told me it makes the cows' breath stink."

"I didn't ask you, did I?" she said, taking a clip at his head, but catching only at the sun-dried strands of his hair.

Matteo bent over beside them and pointed to some small clusters of velvety soft ovals. "But do you know what these are?" he asked, crushing one in his fingers and holding it under their noses.

Marcus spoke up first. "That smells like toothpaste. You gonna eat that too?"

Matteo laughed. "I'm going to eat that too!" He stood up. "Come with me. Here, Ruth Ann." He handed her the basket. "You should carry this. You will look like a princess."

She pouted. "No. Princesses don't carry baskets of old weeds nor nothing else."

"They do in some stories," he said.

She considered this, then took the basket and headed off in front of the others.

In a short while they reached an open space where the main road connecting their houses swept in a curve shaded by a cluster of locust trees. Matteo sat on one of the green-grey rocks that had been heaped along the roadside, forming a bulwark against wandering cows. Without knowing why, the children took their places expectantly on either side of him. The blue dust of the road hung in little drifts on the leaves of the plants, under which grasshoppers filed their legs together noisily. Beyond them, over the fields opposite, the tin roof of a distant farmhouse sparkled in the sunlight, like a square burning star nestled in a cove of trees. The silence of the afternoon trembled wistfully on the glass-like wings of a bumblebee poised above a cornflower.

Ruth Ann was the first to speak. "What we sitting here for?"

Matteo looked at her, and at the yellowed stem of a locust-tree leaf that had caught itself unobserved in the pocket of her shirt.

"We're waiting," he said.

"For what?"

"For you to pick us some flowers to take home."

She looked around at the sprays of colour that flecked and dotted the tall withered shafts of grass.

"There ain't no flowers here. Them's just weeds."

Matteo looked sad. He got up and went across the road to a place where a jade-coloured plant grew from among the stones. He picked off a dense flock of blossoms the colour of a shadowed sky, and laid it carefully on the basket.

"How about these?" he asked.

Marcus jumped down from the stones and looked around him. There, twining up the tree was a vast coil of flowers as purple as a king's robe. He pulled down a long vinous rope of them and heaped them on the basket.

"But they'll all be dead by morning," Ruth Ann protested.

"Then I shall pick more tomorrow," Matteo answered, breaking off the base of a huge orange lily.

In five minutes the basket was completely hidden under a heap of yellow, orange, blue and white blossoms, and Matteo led them up the hill towards his house.

Once inside, he set the basket on the kitchen table and went to a cupboard to find water glasses for himself, his friends, and their flowers. Before they knew it, the children were over the threshold and a secondary shyness suddenly overcame them.

They both remained standing beside the basketful of plants, as though clinging to a familiar friend. Matteo silently handed them each a glass of water, and gestured for them to go outside to the porch. Once there, both children immediately leapt on to the swing, and with their feet swaying to and fro, set it in motion. Observing through the window, Matteo wondered if they had ever sat there before. After a while he joined them, seating himself just beyond their reach of their swinging feet and gazing at the valley below.

"How come we ain't drinking wine?" Marcus asked.

"Sully!"

"Because we are too thirsty," Matteo answered. "Thirsty people should only drink water." It was something Nonna had always told him, and he had heard his mother repeat it.

"Oh," Marcus answered. He thought for a moment. "You drink wine a lot? You ever get drunk?"

"*Sully!*"

"Well, you wanted to know too, when Pa told us about all them boxes being delivered and all," Marcus told his sister.

"I don't get drunk," Matteo answered. His mother had been strictly teetotal since her return to Italy, and the abhorrence with which she spoke of all drink made him shun it as well until he went to university. "It's good to drink a little, I think. In Italy, it's a part of life."

"Oh." Marcus answered, more confused than ever.

"What's it like in them places?" Ruth Ann asked. She sipped her water and licked her lips, as if it were wine.

"It's beautiful, like here. And it's warm, like here. The people are very friendly, and they go to church a lot. They like to have their families all living close together—like here, and that's why it was so hard for my Mama to leave there to come here. It's why I couldn't come here sooner to see this place again."

Marcus spoke up. "Daddy says you was born here, so it's natural that you come back to see it again, cause you was a boy here, like me."

Ruth Ann looked at him hopefully with rounded eyes. "You going to stay here awhile?"

Marcus added, "You could get married and stay here and have some kids like us, and we could play and that would be real fun."

"We go to church a lot, too," Ruth Ann added.

"Yeah and people here's friendly too, except there ain't nobody to play with much, and there ain't nothing to do."

"What you do when you was a boy here?"

Matteo sighed. The depth of feeling in the children's words touched him. He stood up. "I used to have things to play with," he said.

The children fell silent as he left the porch and disappeared into the house. After a moment, there was a thudding on the stairs and he returned with his arms wrapped around a huge green canvas army bag. He carefully lowered the bag to the porch floor, and undid the drawstrings.

"Here," he said, "I think you ought to look inside for yourselves."

The children hopped down off the swing and in a flash their hands tugged the mouth of the bag open. A small wooden bowling pin, an elephant, and a clown seated in a car tumbled on to the planked floorboards. Both the children gasped.

With precision and care, they drew the contents of the bag out into the daylight, one piece at a time. There were small red cars and large yellow trucks; black cows, snow white hens and buff-coloured pigs; an entire world for playing, piling, sorting, and throwing.

Soon, the air hummed with the purr of motors formed by

small lips. A dog pulled by a string chased a cat whose mouth opened and closed in never-ending wooden meows. Footsteps pounded along the boards as planes soared into flight, held aloft by little hands. There was a royal blue boat with a cotton sail; blocks painted in rainbow shades; the gloved hands of the marionette clapped and his jaw rose and sank in silent speech. There was abundance and there was busy, busy joy as Matteo took a seat on the porch-swing to watch.

What puzzled him about the children's reactions to this treasure horde was the way they examined each toy meticulously before playing with it. He guessed that there was nothing in the bag (apart from the costumed marionette and the circus animals) that they had not seen in real life, and yet each thing they picked up held them fascinated for minutes before they consented to make it part of some game.

Their fingers smoothed around and around over the shiny surfaces, and their nails picked at the scratches left from the hours of Matteo's own childhood. There was nothing they did not examine, nothing that satisfied them without the company of thought.

After arranging the tiny silver poles of a circus cage into its board, Marcus spent several minutes adjusting the posture of its captive lion, before he was prepared to turn his attention to something else. Neither child spoke, though at times their hands were inches apart. The toys had cast a spell over them, and there was no room for concerns beyond the imagination.

"Are these like your own toys?" Matteo asked.

"No, we ain't got this many. But yeah, they're a little like them," Marcus answered.

"No, they ain't," said Ruth Ann.

Matteo was interested. "What makes them different?"

"Well, ours ain't made of wood like these," Marcus said.

"No," Ruth Ann said, looking at a crank-powered windmill. "I mean, ours ain't this kind of wood, but these is, I don't know ... just different." She grabbed one of the windmill's turning blades and looking up to smile at Matteo. "For one thing, ours ain't got these on them." And she ran her finger over a peculiar circle of paint.

"Yeah," Marcus agreed, "but them's just pictures. That ain't nothing special."

Ruth Ann was triumphant. "Oh, yes they are!"

"No, they ain't."

Ruth Ann said nothing else, but her finger traced again and again the little disc of colour.

Matteo was intrigued by her careful attention. The girl was very sure of herself. The design was repeated on all of the toys he could see before him, the largest one visible on either side of the Ferris wheel.

Matteo picked up the wheel and gave it a spin. As he watched, the geometric design yielded a misty impression of concentric circles. When the wheel stopped turning, he studied the arrangement carefully. Lop-sided blue, green and yellow squares and triangles, four equidistant black dots, and in the centre, one simple red rectangle: a pattern he had taken for granted all his life, yet never really stopped to study.

He surveyed the other toys around the room. Wherever there was space—on the wheels of the cars, on the saddles of the horses, on the clowns' hats—the pattern was repeated. He had always thought of it as a plain abstraction, a sort of cryptic sigil that his father had given the toys when he had completed their construction. Recalling that he had seen similar ones on the sides of a nearby barn, he was troubled.

"So, Ruth Ann, what's special about these little pictures?"

The girl looked at him with wide eyes, and a finger a-twirl in her hair. She grinned. "Them's hex signs. And they're magic."

"No they ain't!" Marcus said.

"Yes they are. They're like a blessing to keep the devil off. You just don't know *nothing.*"

She took the Ferris wheel from Matteo and gave it a spin. When the little rings of colour slowed once again into the neat and orderly pattern, Marcus picked up a yo-yo and looked hard at the design. Then he went and leaned against one of the porch posts, biting his lip in defeat.

Ruth Ann's words didn't bother Matteo—he had known folk superstitions all his life, and was both relieved and amused to discover some meaning in the mysterious designs. Still, he felt sorry for Marcus.

Victorious in her argument but deprived of her playmate, Ruth Ann up-ended the bag and was rewarded with a shower of dozens and dozens of little dark brown ovals, hard as nails. She picked one up and examined it before tossing it at Marcus.

It struck his ear and he winced. "Ow!"

Marcus recovered the projectile and made ready to pelt his sister in turn, but Matteo held out his hand, gesturing for Marcus to hand it over.

"Yeah, dummy," Ruth Ann said. "Don't you be throwing no old beans at me!"

Matteo cupped the little oval that Marcus had given him. "What did you call them?"

Ruth Ann picked up another one and squeezed it. "Aw, they're some kind of old bean or other. They're just dried up 'cause they're so old."

"These ain't no beans," Marcus said quietly, stuffing a few into his pocket.

"Oh, yes they are, ain't they, Matthew?"

Matteo looked at the small, hard pellet he held, and then at the porch floor where the rest lay scattered among the host of bright toys, a constellation of seeds. He swept up a handful, trying to remember. Why had he kept them? Were they something he had played with as a boy?

"I don't know what they are," he said.

Ruth Ann *humphed* dismissively, and looked again at Marcus. "Well, go on then, smarty-pants, what are they then, if they ain't beans?"

"I ain't a-saying," Marcus mumbled.

His sister took this as an invitation to taunt him. With quiet cunning, she pursued him around the porch, interrupting him when he tried to play with the toys, tickling his neck, tweaking his hair and ears.

Matteo wished she would stop, but had no idea how to make her. Never having witnessed behaviour like this, he was at a loss to know what to do—especially as the outburst of bullying appeared to be completely unprovoked. Yet Marcus went on stoically examining each toy one by one, pausing to trace the outlines of the hex signs.

All at once, the trouble stopped. Ruth Ann dropped the only one of the little oblongs she still held, then looked at Matteo and shrugged her shoulders. "Well, I guess there ain't no use trying. I might as well get on home before I get into trouble. Bye, Matthew."

And with that, she walked off.

Matteo watched her go in silence, then sat down in the porch swing. Marcus patiently re-arranged the toys into play-order. He drew together the scattered farm animals, returned the people to the carousel, and tucked the jack-in-the-box safely into its lair. When everything was tidy, he used his hand to sweep together the scattered brown dots that had so provoked his sister.

Matteo scooted off the swing and sat down on the floor beside him, then held open the canvas bag for Marcus to put them away. Out of sight and out of mind.

Standing up, Marcus took the last of the black pellets from

his pocket and dropped it into Matteo's hand. His eyes were strangely sad, and his voice had a catch in it when he spoke.

"That's a pawpaw seed," he said, then turned away to sit once more beside the bag of toys.

Matteo's lips silently formed the foreign word, then he asked Marcus to say the name again.

Marcus muttered the sound under his breath, then stood up and stepped down off the porch. He went slowly around the corner and settled himself down with his back against the trunk of the dogwood tree where Matteo had discovered the little box. Over his head, the sunlight was winnowed by the fan of leaves. A faint draught of honeysuckle blossom steeped the air with scent. Matteo followed him and sat down, his back against the same tree, but facing the other way.

Marcus was the first to speak. "Ain't nothing."

"What isn't?"

"A pawpaw. Its just a kind of thing like a pear, except littler and real soft inside. They grow on trees, and they're green mostly. When they get ripe, they go kind of brown, and ya pick them and eat them. Girls don't like them cause ya got to spit a lot."

"Why do you have to spit a lot?"

"Cause they're so dern full of seeds, that's why."

"Are they special?" Matteo asked.

"Aw, I don't know. I doubt it. Not to most folks." Marcus was breaking-up little sticks with his fingers and throwing them one-by-one at a spider three feet from his shoe.

"Are they special to some people?"

No answer.

"Are they magic? Really magic?"

Marcus's chin drooped a little and he spoke very quietly. "Sometimes when there ain't nobody 'round, I seen Daddy go and sit under one. He just sits there and sits there till he starts to bawl. Then he just gets up and goes on home and don't never tell nobody."

Uncomfortable and unhappy, Matteo reached around the tree and laid his hand on the boy's shoulder. "And don't you tell anybody either. Everybody has a secret. That's fair. I mean, I don't think you want me to know what a … pawpaw tree looks like, do you?"

Marcus stood up excitedly. "Well sure ya can! I'll…" He stopped. Matteo was smiling, and Marcus was back to his old self. "I'll show ya right now, if ya want."

He stepped forward and pointed at a place midway up the opposite slope to a small, half-grown-over clearing. "There's lots of them in there."

Matteo strained to see the place. There must have been hundreds of trees in the general area, most of which he did not know.

"Maybe you can show me up close?" Matteo scanned the intervening divide, calculating the shortest way, but before they could set out he spotted movement: two figures, coming closer. As the pair neared the house, he saw it was Ruth Ann, walking with a purposeful stride and leading her altogether more reluctant father.

"Come on," Matteo said. "We'll go and meet them."

They cut across the hillside and met Ruth Ann and Jonas at the fence between the two properties.

"Hey, Matthew!" Jonas shouted. "That boy of mine still working for ya, and educating ya about stuff that ain't worth knowin'?"

Jonas sounded cheerful, and Matteo felt a sudden wave of relief. Until this moment he had not realised how uneasy the discovery of the hex signs and paw-paw seeds had made him.

"Hello, Jonas. Marcus and Ruth Ann have helped me to

gather some of my supper. As a reward, I've shown them some of my old toys."

"Yeah, Ruthie done said you sure got lots of stuff. Listen, if them two does get in your way, you just send them on home, ya hear? Ruth told me she and that one there had words, and it ain't fitting that they squabble around you." He laughed. "What with you being without any kids of your own and all, I expect you want to keep the peace as long as ya can."

Matteo felt certain that Ruth Ann had tried to stir up some trouble for her brother, and that Jonas had broken into his day, had come up the hill on this errand, solely to keep the peace. Marcus, still on Matteo's side of the fence, looked up at him.

"Don't worry, Jonas," Matteo said, "they are no trouble. I like to have them about, and toys need to be played with. Anyway, the things they show me are as good as the things I show them. I teach them to eat grass, and they show me where to step and where not to step."

Jonas nodded. "You want their company, you're welcome to 'em." He looked at the children, who had now moved down the lane and were examining some flowering weeds. "But you two best get on back to the garden and get on with what you was supposed to be doing. Ya hear?"

The two children ran towards home, raising a plume of dust with their feet, and Ruth Ann filling the silent shade with tiny squeals as Marcus bombarded her with daisy heads.

Chapter Five

Orange-gilt maple leaves — cloths torn from an autumn basket — furl and unfurl on the firm air of the morning. Matteo's boots, muddied, dusted and muddied again grit softly over the ploughed fields as he makes his way up the hillside opposite the valley from his house.

Grey squirrels, tails twitching in silver flashes through the leaves beneath the walnut trees, stop and stare at him full-faced, then bound away on errands of their own, anxious to prepare for the shadows of winter. Wire fences squeak shrilly in the silence as he crosses them. A trail of frost warmed into dew marks the path he takes over the stubbled margins of corn. His destination lies at the end of a child's distant finger-point; its shape — like its character — is a question that lingers before him.

At last he pauses and lays his hand on the rings of a small

grubby tree stump, marvelling at the mountainside dressed in motley.

A pool of lavender mist hung over the grooves where the streams, long since drained by the hot days, were at last re-filling. Greenish black circles like damp stains marked the spots where clusters of cedars grew, and Matteo heard the stammering of wings as a murder of crows rose over uncut and unharvested fields.

The loneliness of the season nested in the hollow places of Matteo's heart as he remembered the people he had loved, and would never see again.

He turned back to the hillside and moved further around its eastern side where the play of light was stronger. In front of him was a pile of blasted and shapeless rocks, discarded because of their unfitness for building. Behind them—bordering the forest that came down to the field's edge—stood another copse of small trees, black with twigs, and knee-deep in their own leaves.

He clambered onto the rocks and sat on the uppermost one, feeling it shift with his weight. The area was littered with small broken sticks; curious to see if they were still green, Matteo bent to pick one up.

As he held it up to the rising light for examination, his gaze re-focussed to discover he could see his own house clearly from where he sat.

On the hill opposite him, the sun was brighter; the mist had fallen away and everything was whitened with reflected sunlight. The house, silhouetted as the day grew behind it, seemed like a child's plaything. From this distance, all appeared happy and peaceful and benign.

The rising contours beyond his house bristled with wild green trees and scattered undergrowth. His eye traced the lane from his front porch as it flowed down to the road where, near the last visible turning, he could see Jonas's home. It was strange, he thought, that this perspective, so clear to him now, should have been hidden from him before.

He looked around, wondering if there were any pawpaw trees nearby, or whether he had misunderstood Marcus's directions. He stood again and went into the cluster of waste growth that separated the pile of rocks from the forest-edge. Leaning on the wire, he saw the colourless profile of a bird swooping to the forest floor, where it scratched for a moment and buried its head among the leaves before re-emerging with a trembling many-legged insect.

Matteo inhaled the tangy scent of resin and studied the timber nearest him, probing his memory for the names of the trees. He counted three types of oak from where he stood, and spotted poplar and sycamore and something that might have been either cherry or plum, and a stand of what he now knew to be locust trees, but there were just as many that he could not name.

With a certain melancholy, mixed with the oddest feeling that he should laugh at himself, Matteo turned around again, thinking that he would go back to his seat on the rock, to enjoy the growing sunshine for a while longer.

To his astonishment, he saw the gold-traced outline of a woman sitting on the very rocks he had left only moments before. Her face was turned towards the valley's incline, and a sudden blaze of sunlight-fire picked out the line of her features from jaw to hair's end. It was Esther.

Her lips were pursed slightly against the cool breeze, and the willowy fringe of her dress lapped softly against the stones and dried vines. For a moment, he thought she might be lost in a daydream, but her face was expressionless and Matteo believed that all dreaming left its imprint on the features.

For a long moment, he stood motionless with indecision. A place, a look, a feeling that made her suddenly beautiful, buried itself like an arrowhead in his chest.

How could he make himself known to her without it seeming that he had followed her, or as if he were skulking aimlessly in the woods? As he pondered the matter, he realised that if she simply turned around and saw him, it would seem even worse. He resolved to make a noise that wouldn't startle her, as though he had just that instant noticed her arrival.

He took the axe up from beside his hip, and swung it lazily at a tiny summer-born sapling. With a feathery snip it whirred into the heap of leaves that lay blown against the tree. He then took aim at a larger sapling, raised the axe over his head, drawing breath as he always did. Holding the axe ready, he glanced at her from the corner of one eye.

Esther leapt up and whirled around, peering among the trees until she had seen him. *"Wholwee!"* She ran the back of her wrist across her brow. "I heard something breathing and I thought you was some kind of animal or something."

"I'm sorry," Matteo said earnestly, striding towards her. He went into the brighter tangle of grass that surrounded the rocks and she sat down again.

"What you doing 'round here?"

It was the question he'd hoped she might not ask. "Looking for a pawpaw tree. Marcus said they grow here."

"Uh-huh." She seemed sceptical. "What ya going to do when ya find one, cut it down?" She laughed.

Relieved, Matteo laughed as well. "No. Are you alone?" Instantly, he regretted the way the question sounded.

"Yeah." She glanced towards her home. "They've all gone down to Daddy's to see his new calves." She turned back to Matteo, smiling. "You by yourself?"

"Yes."

"You can sit down, unless ya got something ya want to be doing. Don't let me run ya off."

She swung a little sideways, drawing back her legs to the

stones at her feet. Matteo sat down on the ground, anxious to appear at ease yet unwilling to share her boulder.

His eyes roamed over the brown arches of Jonas's fields, groomed to lie fallow for the winter. "I never guessed that you could see so much from up here. It doesn't look possible from down below."

"Yeah, it's real nice. Jonas likes to come up here sometimes. We used to walk up here a lot when we was just starting out. You know, just looking at things. Things we wanted to do and all. This has been Jonas's place for years. His people had it, and he worked it alone practically since he was a boy. He loves it 'round here. His people's buried down there the other side of them trees."

Matteo was silent.

Esther prodded his shoulder gently with her foot. "Now don't you just sit there like a bump on a log. Them kids of mine think you're the best thing since sparks made fire."

He smiled and looked up at her. "Oh? What have they said? That I eat grass and spend the whole day drinking wine?"

"Well, it ain't polite to say." She tucked a stray lock of hair behind one ear, laughing mischievously.

"They're good children," Matteo said, "but sometimes Ruth Ann teases Marcus too much."

"Yeah, she's hateful to him, ain't she? Just like me and her daddy."

Matteo wondered at this remark, but said nothing.

"I expect they done told you all about us, but I don't know nothing about you except you got a whole lot of toys and stuff. Them your toys, or what?"

"Yes, my father made them for me when I still lived here."

"Oh. What you gonna do with them?"

"I don't know."

"Your mama was Italian, wasn't she?"

"That's right."

"And when your daddy was killed she went on home to her people and took you with her?"

"Yes."

"Oh."

Matteo saw a flicker in her eyes as she looked at him. Then she turned away to gaze across the fields. "What's it really like in them places? Is folks different? I bet things look different, don't they? Must look something like this though, don't it?"

Her curiosity made him uneasy. His plan, before he came here, had been to say as little as possible in response to such questions, even though he knew they were inevitable. Partly, this was because he'd hoped to appear mysterious, tormenting the asker of the question. Partly, it was because he didn't know the answers himself. But he remembered how open he had been with Marcus, and tried to do the same now.

"Yes, it is very like this. Except at night. When you lie awake at night there, if you listen very carefully you can hear the waves of the sea. The forests there have more large trees in them, and I think that people use them more. I mean there are many nut trees. The farms grow mostly the same things—corn, hay, wheat. Maybe more vegetables, I don't know. There are many orchards, some with lemons and oranges, and where the land is not so good there are olives. Oh yes, and vines, for grapes, to make wine. It is very hot in the summer, like here, but I don't think it's as cold in the winter. I cannot remember any snow, except here. My village is much bigger than this, and most of the houses are closer together. There are more places to buy things, but I think not as many things to buy. We have one church only, and the priest is a very nice man who grows very large sweet chickpeas. For most of the time I lived with my mother and grandparents. Nonna—that's my grandmother—was very special. When I was a boy she used to bake little sweet cakes with nuts in them. I would carry them in my pockets to school while they were still warm from the oven. Nonno used to say — he was my grandfather — that there was nothing that Nonna couldn't do except lose an argument. Nonno was very special, too. He taught me almost everything I didn't learn in school. Well, except for Mama. Mama used to laugh and make me tell her everything. But that's just what boys don't want to do. Nonno never asked me anything. I wanted to be like him."

Matteo fell silent.

"Well?" Esther asked.

"There isn't much else. I went to school. I did the things that most boys do. Except that when I was old enough, I went to university."

"What about when ya grew up? What do the grown-up Italians do? What did your granddaddy do?"

No one had ever asked Matteo such personal questions in such a frank manner. He sighed and shifted to a more comfortable position against the cold stone. "After the war, a lot of people made money. So did Nonno. After he died, there was no one left but me. I thought I would like to take some time to see ... to do ... something different. Something I knew, but couldn't remember." He fidgeted. "Other people are different. I don't know. Their families, their jobs..." He straightened up, putting a brave face on a feeling he didn't like. "I'm young. There's still time to ... look at things."

"How old are you?"

"Twenty-five," he said.

Esther laughed. "Well, sir, most of the fellers 'round here is done married and feathered their nests by that time."

Matteo forced a tight grin on to his face.

"Ain't ya got no girl?" she asked.

He looked away. She waited a moment, then continued: "I mean, it's alright wanting to get to know yourself and all. I guess if I was born there, then lived here mostly, I'd want to go there for a while to see it. 'Specially if I had the money. But you got to be thinking. I mean you're going to have to settle down some time, and ya ain't never going to know when, and ya ain't never going to know with who. So ya got to get a little ready. I suppose you ain't even made up your mind where ya want to be yet. But you sure ought to be thinking."

Matteo was certainly thinking. Neither his mother, nor Nonna, had ever advised him to hurry through his life. Their advice had always been to go as slowly as possible.

"I mean, ya ain't getting any younger. Ain't Italian girls pretty?"

His mind flashed back to an afternoon in Perugia...

Errant shafts of blinding sunlight pierced the cellar-like darkness of a tiny alley as he hurried along with his friend. Pools of water stood like linked chains in the gutters, and a funnel of steam rose from a laundry hatch below his knee. As he looked into the corridor of broken light and shade, a door opened in front of him. A woman in a cream and tan dress emerged, her back towards him. As she stepped backward into a column of sunlight, her hair seemed to tingle with firelight. Suddenly aware of the two young men who had stopped — open-mouthed — to let her pass by, she turned towards them. Then she smiled.

More than her smile, more than her eyes, even more than the graceful comb of her cheek, it was her eyebrow that he remembered, for as her eyes met Matteo's, she lifted one delicate arch.

It was that tiny gesture—granted in the late summer of his final undergraduate year—that gave Matteo the confidence to believe in his future as a man to whom love might one day be given. And it was for that feeling that he waited.

"There's still time," he said at last. "There must be."

"Uh-huh. Don't ya want some kids?"

He was steadier now. "Of course! Some day I will meet someone, and for her I will…"

He stopped. She was looking at him strangely.

"Sing a song?" she asked.

"I will sing many songs."

"Them two of mine sure like to hear you sing. Ya ought to go to church. We could do with a feller who don't mind singing in front of folks." She sighed. "But you're just like Jonas. He used to sing to me sometimes. Not that he could sing, ya understand, but I liked it. He's older than me, ya know."

She looked away, far down over the fields, and Matteo saw the ladder of years in her mind. "He was sure something. He worked like a dog at this place, all the day and half the night. After his mammy died, nobody never saw him 'round much, he worked so hard. I mean, it don't look like much to you, I reckon, but it's a lot for one feller to do. Nobody did nothing for him. He used to go down to the shop sometimes in the evening, after the milking, and his arms would be as black as tea from working in the sun. It's not that nobody didn't like him or nothing, it's just that he was on his own, and everybody knew it, and nobody knew what to say to him. I liked him cause he was kind of shy-like, and he never teased nobody much. The other fellers threw him in the crick once, and when he pulled his self out he took his shirt off and, well, he was all white down to the neck and shoulders, cause he never took his shirt off outside. Them boys give him a time for that, and I felt sorry for him, ya know. Well, he used to talk to me sometimes, then one day he said he wanted to marry me, and that he had thought about it a lot his own self, and he'd do anything for me, and never mind what anybody said, and if I wanted to see the farm and all, I should bring somebody with me an he'd show us all 'round. He was so nice—nicest any feller had ever been to me, that I just knew it would be alright. And it is. He loves them kids more than anybody knows, and he still works like a dog, only there ain't so much to do now. I still reckon he'd do anything for me." She looked at Matteo. "Yep, he's just like you."

Matteo heard this story with real feeling. Any story of love opened up something inside him, something that fed and starved at the same time—a curiosity about himself and his future.

He looked happily across the fields to a small herd of cows grazing in the meadow near the lane. "Nonno told me once that there was a man in our village who had loved a woman ever since he had been a child. When this man was a boy he had stood on a stone in the wall to watch her as she hung out her laundry, and sometimes, when he felt very brave, he picked wildflowers and left them on her doorstep. He also sometimes left her presents of tomatoes, or little wedges of cheese wrapped up in paper. She was a widow, Nonno said, and like most widows, she hated living alone, and she wanted very much to know who it was who left her these presents. She asked everyone in the village, but no one knew who her mystery lover could be. So, one night, when the boy was about twelve, he went to her house after dark to leave her a basket of apricots. When he turned to go away, she heard his footsteps on the stones and suddenly opened her window and called to him. 'Boy,' she said, 'who is your master?' 'I have no master,' he answered. 'Then from whom do you bring these presents?' And the boy replied, 'From someone who loves you—someone you look at, but cannot see.' Well, no more presents came, and the widow thought about this for a long time. Years went by, and there was a war with the French. Then one day, a soldier brought her a gift. 'Is this your name?' he asked, showing her the address he had been sent to. She looked hard at the writing, for she had grown old, and could not see as well as she used to. 'Yes,' she said, at last. 'Then I must give you these,' the soldier replied, and he handed her a pair of cavalryman's spurs. 'They once belonged to my captain. Before he died, he asked me to bring them here.' The widow touched her heart, for she knew then that the boy who had given her the terrible answer to her question had loved her for the sake of the man he would become."

Finished with his story, Matteo felt a wave of pure happiness wash over him. It always brought him peace to think of simple things and lasting love. He turned towards Esther, and she too was smiling. She sighed. "Well, sir, I reckon you're just like that boy *and* that widow."

Matteo's contentment fell away like rain. A moment before, he hadn't thought that he was like either of them. "I don't understand," he said.

"Well, some folks just got to do some things in a certain way. You got to think about things. Jonas is just like that. He thinks about everything. Things get right down inside him and they just sit there till he's done with them. He won't sleep. He worries about dern near everything. 'When's it going to stop raining? Ain't it going to rain soon?'"

"But he's a farmer," Matteo said, eager to defend his friend. "Farmers have a lot to worry about. They work hard, they…"

In one fluid movement, Esther slid off the rock and took several steps forward, hands on hips. "Oh, he don't need to worry that much. And he sure don't need to work all the time."

Matteo could tell by her stance that she was vexed, and he looked for a way to turn aside from this open door that led to a private darkness. "So, he works. But he has made it beautiful. And the children…"

"He says he does it all for me. All *what* for me? He works cause that's all he knows. He works 'cause he wants something, or he's afraid of something. And there ain't nothing wrong. I tell him over and over that there ain't nothing wrong, and he says it too, and he just goes on working like the whole damn world's waiting for him to do a little more. And it's even got in to them kids. They want something. They always go 'round looking for something, and they don't know what. They follow him 'round, a-watching to see what he's going to do next, cause there's sure to be something else to do. Now they all talk about you morning noon and night. 'Ain't nobody can swing a axe like that feller can! Ain't nobody never sung songs like he does, and in some foreign language.' I tell ya, a body works all day, and when the night comes, all ya want is a little peace. Just a feeling that, well, that much is done. But they're … they're all looking for more. They see something in everything—something to do, something to make, something to talk about. Something so tomorrow won't go away. Something they got to get 'round to before tomorrow can come."

She spun on her heel to face him, and Matteo saw that the light that had graced her had now fallen away and her face was now moulded in planes and angles of shadows.

"Ya know, if I was to give you some advice, what I'd tell ya is to get on back out of here before ya get some of it in you too. There's something about living 'round here that just gets in to people and makes them funny. They believe stuff that nobody nowheres else believes in. They go on a-working when there ain't no work to do. And they know stuff they ain't never going to tell, cause they don't know they know it. Now them kids of mine think you're something, and I guess ya are. I'm glad, real glad. But it's just something else for Jonas to worry about. And when you're done doing whatever it is your doing, I expect you'll go away, and we'll all talk about ya, cause ya was different and we liked ya and all. But Jonas'll just keep on a-thinking, wondering why he ain't like you, same as he ain't like other fellers. Then he'll start to wonder why I married him, and go out and do some more work, or something. And he'll start to think them kids liked you better than him, then I don't know what-all."

Matteo felt Esther's words cover him slowly, then sink into

his skin like a bitter perfume that soured his heart. How much folly and pain and unanswered longing there was in the love story she told. How strange it sounded, how strange that it could be told. Yet what strangeness had there been between his own mother and father?

Was the laughter, and the tenderness of fingers that laced and unlaced on the windowsill, only a portion of a language so private that none but they understood, because none but they could know the loneliness and the joy that had fused between them? Had Nonno loved in a way too secret for words, too secret for anything but a look that only Nonna could read? Something in Esther's words was so profound and so resolute that he was moved to respect husband and wife as sharing something more than love, something more like inspiration.

Esther kicked his shoe. "Stop it, now. It don't matter, and I sure don't need you to start worrying like the rest of them."

He nodded his head but said nothing.

"Bet you didn't expect nothing like all this, did ya? Well, I told ya, folks 'round here's funny. You just go on singing and all. Ruth Ann and Marcus can't get enough of ya, and Jonas can sure do with the help. You can come 'round to supper any time, and if ya need anything for that house of yours, you just ask me, ya hear?"

She started off down the hillside with a buoyant nonchalance. All at once, she stopped, and ran back towards him.

"Oh yeah," she sputtered laughingly and a little out of breath. "Them scrubby little trees ya was a-chopping at — them's pawpaw trees. That's as big as they get, and sometimes they got fruit and sometimes they don't."

She turned homeward again, and Matteo — sore-throated from silent and sustained tension — watched her walk into the distance, measuring with his eye the long flat shadow that the day threw behind her.

Chapter Six

A very small nose presses against a window, pinpoints of cold tingling over it. On either side, above it and below, there are others — seven in all. Matteo's young neighbours have come to watch him at work.

Behind them, the tousle of autumn has vanished, and in its place winter holds the forest in its claws. So hard has the ground frozen that the push of their boots on the glazed-over snow sings shrilly with every step. Skies once invisible to the forest floor float in featureless grey above the tops of the trees. Unfiltered by any softness, the ruthless wind brushes the children's faces like callused hands. In the silence beyond the scrape of their feet, the children listen to the strange, slow sounds of Matteo's tools as he shapes a piece of wood.

The softened and decayed furniture that had once been a feature of his family's parlour was now upstairs, in the timbered loft of the house's huge attic. In its place, Matteo had built a row of cupboards, some shelves, a bench, a stool and a crude chair, and a large workbench, above which hung many of his new tools. The open shelves, full to bursting, glinted with wildly assorted swirls of colours, like flowers in a shop window, and it was here that most of the children fixed their eyes.

They saw tiny carousels and windmills, miniature farm-yards filled with animals of every description; a stack of jig-saw puzzles, blocks, rattles, an open jack-in-the-box — more things than the children could have easily counted. None of these things were surprises — Ruth Ann and Marcus had made certain that Matteo's legend preceded him — and yet by their strange combination of contour, texture and colour, they were toys that made the observers shiver with fascination and joy.

Those children who peered beyond the toys saw Matteo seated comfortably with his back to the window and in the centre of a dense, yolk-gold triangle of light cast by the lamp on the workbench. On the bench behind his shoulder stood a long tall boat, without sails, but holding a narrow barn-like house. The bottom of the boat was painted blue, its walls yel-low, and its roof red, picked-out with white detailing. On the bench and floor were pairs of wooden animals — lions, geese, elephants, pigs — all grouped around Matteo and watching, like the children, as he worked a lump of sugary pine with a short hooked knife.

The animal he was carving was only half-finished. Its bot-tom half was still solid, but on top — as the children looked on with wonder — Matteo shaped a long thin neck.

"A giraffe," Marcus whispered.

"No it ain't," Ruth Ann replied.

"Well, what is it then?"

Ruth Ann was silent a moment, thinking hard. "A flamin-go," she said at last.

"What's that?"

"A pink bird. They got them in Florida, in the swamps or something."

With a sudden movement, Matteo laid aside his work, stood up and crossed the room to the wood-stove, then crouched to open the hatch and add more fuel from the pile in the corner. As he stirred the seething cake of embers, the children instinctively breathed deeply as a puff of summer-sweet smoke moved above their heads.

Standing some way away from the other children was a little boy with blonde curly hair and sage-blue eyes. Only five years old, he was the youngest and smallest of the group, and since he could only just see through the window by standing on his toes, he didn't really know what he was supposed to be watching, though he had an unquenchable urge to get at the toys. His feet were hardening with cold and the smell of the smoke proved to be too much. It went straight through his nostrils, disturbed all of his taste buds, and swam uncomfortably around his stomach, from whence it re-emerged as a loud complaint.

"I'm hungry!"

All six of his colleagues' heads turned to offer a fierce "*Shh!*" but it was too late. On the dry empty air of the woods, the little notes of his voice went straight through the walls, and Matteo heard them.

Over the past few months he had grown accustomed to his neighbours turning up singly or in groups to offer him help, advice, criticism, turnips and what-not, but he did not expect to hear the sound of a child complaining of want immediately outside his window. As he walked to the window, Matteo was just in time to see a larger child grab the little boy by the scarf—nearly throttling him—and attempting to drag him away amid the latter's shouts of, "Get off! Get off!"

A rush of noises that sounded like a stampede on broken

crackers, together with a web of tiny prints in the ice-crusted snow, made it instantly plain what had happened. Guessing their plans, Matteo ran to his door and out onto the porch against the sudden thrust of the stunningly cold air.

"Hello! Don't be afraid. It's warm inside, and there is coffee and little doughnuts."

As if through enchantment, the scuttling sound of small feet over snow-packed leaves stopped. Two small faces, just visible under orange-dyed hunter's fur caps, appeared around the corner of the porch. Matteo, feeling the freezing air burn against the bare triangle of exposed skin below his neck, smiled at the two boys. He did not know the oldest one, but he had seen the little fellow about before, trailing after Marcus.

"Hello," he said, watching the boy unpick fibres of his scarf from the cracks in his wind-dried lips. "I'm sure that I know you, but I can't remember your name."

The boy was silent, and Matteo tried again.

"Aren't you a friend of Marcus's?"

"Who, me?"

"Hm ... yes. Is this young man your brother?"

The boy looked at his older companion as if he had never seen him before. "No, this is Tommy. We're cousins. Our mothers is sisters," he explained

"Oh, I see." Matteo looked as appreciative as possible. "And what's your name?"

"Sandy Pye," he said, stepping forward as if at school.

Glancing at the stalks of hair protruding from around the boy's cap, Matteo put forth his hand. "So. My name is Matteo, and I'm pleased to meet you."

Sandy tentatively shook his hand.

"Do you like doughnuts, Sandy?" Matteo asked.

"Uh-huh!"

"Me too!" Tommy spoke up enthusiastically.

Matteo tried to keep from laughing, and failed. "Well, fellows, come inside. Do you drink coffee?"

"We ain't never drunk no coffee before."

Matteo turned around, as this voice came from one of three other children who now stood at the end of the porch nearest his lane. Behind them, waving, he saw Marcus and Ruth Ann, jogging down the lane towards their friends, looking for all the world as if they had just that moment arrived.

After he had directed all of his guests into the kitchen—where they quickly took their places on every available seat—he stirred up the fire under the huge whistling kettle that had been his mother's, and took out some cups.

Being offered coffee was one thing, but now as each child looked down at the cups placed before them, the reality that they might actually be given some to drink was almost more than they could stand. Matteo took a round tin down off a shelf from above the door to the stairs and opened it up. Like his grandmother, he always kept a tin full of small cakes in the house, just in case someone came to call. This habit—or rather commitment, as that's what it amounted to—had always mystified his friends, who thought it quaint and provincial. But he had maintained it, even as a student, and still kept it up even though few visitors ever crossed his threshold; most people preferred to call on Matteo when they could see him at work outside.

He set the tin on the table beside of a stack of little plates. The children watched with silent intensity as he placed a tiny, square, hard-sounding parcel on to each and passed them around. Not one of them could resist either touching a bit of the sugary surface then licking their fingers, or picking up the entire thing to nibble at the edge.

Their hesitancy was unexpected, given both their ages and the usual small degree of mannerliness they showed, and Matteo watched them all with some confusion. He wondered if they were afraid. No one simply tucked-in with the vigour he had imagined likely. This quiet rigidity continued even after every cup was brimful of coffee.

He gestured around the table. "Please, do help yourselves."

Some of the children, including Ruth Ann and Marcus, looked shame-faced. One of the boys Matteo didn't know spoke up.

"Ain't we a-going to say grace?"

Suddenly it all became clear to Matteo; even the worry in Marcus's and Ruth Ann's looks. They knew that he never prayed before eating, and he knew that they seldom did. But it was obvious that this was what good manners here demanded.

Thinking fast, Matteo asked the group, "Perhaps one of you will lead?"

"I will," Ruth Ann said, and all the others bowed as she muttered, "God is good, God is gracious, and we thank him for this food. A-men."

It was as though seven bolts of lightning struck seven little cakes. Matteo watched as the diners nibbled, lip-smacked and ruminatively masticated the little pastries. Plainly, they were unlike anything the children had ever encountered, their crunchy hardness melting away to an aromatic nutmeg and aniseed tenderness. From the sounds around the table it was clear the children were delighted. Then came the coffee.

Only Ruth Ann kept up the pretext of being at ease with her drink. After several months of Matteo's ways, she and Marcus were unperturbed by the appearance of such extravagant grown-up generosity, but for the others Matteo's customs of hospitality—like the bite of a forbidden apple—were astonishing. Plainly, not one of the children liked the taste of their drink. Yet all drank it sparingly, savouring it in spite of their revulsion. When all of the cups were at last empty, Matteo looked around the silent table.

As always, Marcus and Ruth Ann had their eyes fixed on his every move, as had little Sandy Pye. The oldest of the others—a boy and a girl—gazed curiously from time to time at the doorway that led ultimately to the workshop.

"Sandy, do you go to church?" Matteo said.

"Yes, sir."

"Have you ever heard of a man named Noah?"

"Yes, sir. He had three boys, like me and Benny and Sam, and a big white beard, just like my granddaddy."

"Hm. And what did he do, this Noah?"

"Well, sir, he built a boat called a ark to hold all the animals in the world, and then it rained for forty days and forty nights, and when it stopped, they all got out again, and there was a rainbow."

"That's right, Sandy. Do you know what an ark looks like?"

"No, sir."

"Would you like to see a little one?"

"Yes, sir."

"Come with me."

Sandy looked around the room, his terror at doing something so utterly new all by himself at war with his consuming curiosity. Slowly, he pushed the chair back from the table, stood, and followed Matteo across the room towards the door of the workroom. As the boy stopped in the doorway, Matteo's head re-appeared above his.

"You can see too," he said to the remaining children. He was answered by the sudden scuff of chairs being pushed back from the table and boots pounding on the wooden floor.

Through a tumble of coffee fumes, creaking leather shoes and damp wool, the children pushed one another into the room. Ruth Ann strode forward alone, while the others—torn

between manners and thrilling anticipation—stood in a
crowd so close that Matteo himself could not move. With her
studied precision, Ruth Ann reached up to a shelf and took
down a jointed wooden doll of a boy with a very long nose.
One by one, she touched the yellow roses painted on his pink
coat, while the others looked on in silence.

The other little girl suddenly squeaked, "That's Pin-OH-
kee-o-uh!" and ran across the room to join Ruth Ann. As the
two of them sat in the farthest corner of the room to examine their find, the boys slowly made their way to the shelves
to investigate. Tommy chose a set of red and white bowling
pins, using the doorway to the kitchen as an alley, and Sandy
Pye pretended to harvest wooden pears and cherries from the
window-sill. Only Marcus seemed ill-at-ease.

Listening to the contented purr and clatter of the children—all of whom had appeared to entirely forget his existence—Matteo sat down again in his place by the workbench,
watched only by the marionette.

He picked up the unfinished flamingo-giraffe. How uncom-
plicated it all was! He would have welcomed a little gentle
music and the presence of someone older than himself to
make the scene complete. He hummed softly and thought of
Nonno. He thought of rolling oranges and roasting chestnuts.
He thought of the winter shoes his village priest used to wear,
and he thought of noises the woodcutters used to swear were
spirits haunting the valleys…

His memories were interrupted by Marcus brushing against
his shoe as the boy pushed himself up on to his toes to have a
closer look at the ark perched on the bench. In his hand Marcus held a small wooden cannon, the solid wheels of which
were adorned with one of the usual hex signs. He was squinting at the pattern on the edges of the roof around the ark's
long house, which appeared to repeat the design on a minute
scale.

Pleased by the thoroughness of the boy's interest, Matteo slid the ark closer to the edge. "Are you looking at the edge of the roof?"

Marcus looked at the wheel he held in his hand, and again at the roof. "I was just checking," he said.

"Checking what?"

"That they was the same."

"They're supposed to be. The little ones are a bit simpler, that's all."

Marcus was quiet, and Matteo was certain now that something was troubling him. "Is anything the matter?" Matteo leaned closer.

"No." He looked at the piece of wood Matteo was holding. "Is that a flum-inguh-ho?"

Matteo laughed. "No, it's a giraffe."

"Oh." Marcus grinned. "How many of them animals ya going to make?"

"I don't know."

"Oh. What others ya going to do?"

"How about some bears?"

"Sure. What else?"

Matteo rubbed his head. "What do you suggest?"

Without hesitation, Marcus walked over to the shelves, near where Sandy Pye knelt building a bridge from some blocks, and pulled out a small piece of wood, shaped a little like a guitar, but flattened on one side and painted black and grey. He brought it back to Matteo. "How about a whole 'nother one of these?"

Matteo took the piece of wood and turned it around several times, looking at it from both front and back. If it was some kind of animal, it was one he had never seen before. Where its eyes should have been, there was a black stripe, and what he supposed was its tail, was also striped black. It was not a toy he recognised, having found it in the room after he moved the furniture out.

"What is it?" he asked Marcus.

Marcus looked incredulous. "Supposed to be a 'coon."

"A what?"

"Aw, ya know, uh rau-KOO-un."

Matteo tried to recall an animal of that name from his past.

"You know," Marcus went on. "Little fellers that live in the places near the cricks and all. People says they wash their food in the water, but I ain't never seen none do it. They got a stripey tail like this, and a little black mask on their faces, like robbers. They only come out at nights."

"Yeah," said Ruth Ann, who now stood near Matteo's elbow, "and they gets rabies a lot, and goes half crazy with it, and people shoot them — right out of the trees."

"I ain't never seen one," the other little girl spoke up.

"Yes, sir," said the larger of the other two boys, who so far had not spoken a word to Matteo. "Our daddy shot one out of a tree too, didn't he Marce?"

"Pee-shirl!" was the only sound the other boy made, along the barrel of an imagined rifle.

"Sully and me could show ya where some might be," suggested Ruth Ann.

"Yeah, yeah," chirruped Maurice and his brother.

"Yeah," said the little girl, running to the kitchen.

"Alright," said Marcus, knitting his brows like his father.

Matteo stood up. "Yes, I think you should show me. I'll get my coat."

Only Sandy Pye sat still, listening to the others roaring away. Returning to the room alone, Matteo looked at the child slowly turning the hands of a wooden clock around and around. He knelt down beside him.

"Ya ain't never going to find no 'coons," the boy said. "They're all asleep now."

"Oh."

"Can I stay here, sir? I ain't never seen so many toys before."

Matteo stroked the boy's head.

"Yes, of course. Will you promise to put a piece of that wood there in the stove, and don't touch the tools?"

"Yes, sir." Sandy smiled. "I'll be good."

Outside, the children scattered down the hillside towards the stream. The bitterness of the mountain winter with its near-solid wind and cutting emptiness was still new to Matteo. He leaned his chin downwards and blew on his hands, feeling the chill already slipping like splinters into his roughened fingers. In the distance he could hear the skirling of an old-fashioned saw-mandrel cutting firewood, and beyond the hillside opposite rose a plume of smoke from a pile of burning brushwood.

Marcus led the way, and before long the entire party swarmed over the stream-side. Matteo had never seen a mountain stream so nearly completely frozen over. Grey-blue ice was capped with peaked white crusts, hiding most of the still-moving water, and the children scrambled along from rock to rock, slipping occasionally, and once or twice breaking through and soaking themselves to the knees as they plunged on without so much as looking about. He thought perhaps the original goal of finding a racoon had long since vanished from their minds, replaced by the simpler pleasure of scudding through the frost-darkened landscape.

As though listening for a cue that Matteo couldn't hear, the entire group halted simultaneously and bent down to examine the ground. Though Matteo looked carefully he could see nothing notable enough to warrant this scrutiny.

They had travelled upstream, into a cup-shaped valley that hooked behind his house and led gradually upwards, ever-steeper, before disappearing into a more sudden V near the mountain's summit. Unlike the stream's typical habit of form-ing a fast, well-cut groove at the base of a depression, this par-ticular spot fanned out widely on both sides, each of which resembled embankments cut into the hillside. The wide circu-lar well these embankments formed sheltered the area from the wind, and made it virtually invisible from outside. Matteo had certainly never noticed it before.

Marcus knelt down in the manner of a work-stiffened older man and examined a snowy patch that lay sheltered by a mesh of dead honeysuckle.

"So, Marcus. Have you found anything?"

"No. These is just muskrat tracks, I think."

Matteo followed the boy's finger towards a constellation of little star-shaped prints in the snow.

"Why do you think there might be, uh, … racoons here?"

"It's got all the things they like. It's quiet, they got plenty of places to hide. And there's a whole lotta things to eat."

Matteo looked around him, unable to fathom how, in this frigid little valley, that could be. "What do racoons eat?" he asked.

"Well, I don't know what-all, but they like rotten stuff, and them's all apple trees 'round there." The boy pointed to the trees whose bare, blackened bark stood out like ink-strokes against the sky.

Matteo, despite his knowledge of forests, was caught off-guard again. He was not accustomed to seeing groves of fruit trees in the depths of the woods. "How did they get there?" he asked, not really meaning for the question to sound as it did.

"Johnny Appleseed planted them." Marcus giggled. "No," he went on. "My daddy says the old fellers used to plant them all 'round the place in the woods to make applejack."

"What's applejack?"

"Aw, I don't know. It's something like moonshine, except they make it with cider."

Not entirely certain what he had just been told, Matteo was curious to learn more. "Is it good?"

"I don't know."

Matteo remembered the local taboo-status of alcohol.

"What does it look like?"

"I ain't never seen it."

"Can I buy some from somebody?"

Marcus turned away as if he hadn't heard, and just then Maurice shouted, "I found a turd!"

The boys all clustered around the discovery and after some discussion, decided it was, after all, the trace of a fox and not a racoon.

"Hey!" a woman's voice called.

Everyone turned to look downstream. It was Esther, closely muffled in an old brown wool coat, and with a pink and green scarf tied snugly under her chin.

None of the children moved or spoke as she approached, except for Tommy who nodded and muttered, "How-do, Miz Farley."

"Yeah, How-do, Tommy Green," Esther replied. "You and Marce is going to be frozen turds yourselves if ya stay 'round here. What you all up to this time?"

Matteo stepped forward, wondering why he felt a little embarrassed. "They were trying to find a racoon to show me," he said.

"Yeah, I done heard all about that. That little runt Sandy Pye said you was gone to find one, and I thought sure enough you'd come here." She regarded Marcus and Ruth Ann. "Now you two get on home, ya hear, 'cause you're going to want your dinner before long."

The two children set off, Ruth Ann turning once to smile farewell to Matteo.

Esther turned to the rest of the group, her voice made shrill by the frost-light air. "As for you others, unless you want to freeze yourselves worse than ya already are, you best get on home too."

The children obeyed, silent and morose. Not one said good-bye.

Esther turned to Matteo with frustration crouched in the lines around her mouth. "Ya know, sometimes I just don't know about you. How long ya been out here? Some of them kids is wet up to the knees, Martha ain't even done her coat up and they all got something they ought to be doing. You're worse than the lot of them." She paused, shaking her head, then smiled. "I knew just where mine would be, alright. 'Gone to see that Matthew.' And I get to your house and there was Sandy sniffing 'round your kitchen looking for I don't know what, holding a little statue of a king or something in his hands proud as ya please. And he said ya gone to find a 'coon, so I knew Marcus would bring ya here."

Taking advantage of the grudging warmth he thought he saw in the light of her brief smile, Matteo asked, "And are there racoons here?"

Esther laughed. "Aw, I reckon. Yeah, all 'round here, 'cause of the water."

"Marcus said they like the fruit from the apple trees."

"I expect so. Since your daddy died, there ain't nobody else wants 'em."

"He used to pick them?"

"Well sure. His daddy's the one that planted them."

Thinking about what Marcus had told him, Matteo was troubled. "But this land isn't mine."

"No, and it weren't your daddy's neither, cause your grand-daddy give it up."

"But whose is it now?"

"Well, it's Jonas's and it ain't worth a damn. Pretty near

every time it rains, the whole thing floods. That's why he don't do nothing with it."

"Did Jonas's father buy it?"

" 'Deed, I don't know just what happened. That's before my time. But it don't matter. If you want any of them apples-the-size-of-cherries next year, you just take them. Jonas'll give ya all ya want."

Then she shook her head, turned and set off for home, leaving Matteo to listen to the prickle of her boot-soles on the leaf-choked snow.

Chapter Seven

Esther Farley was ten years and three months old when her mother taught her the ways to catch and keep the man of her choice. Two days after her tenth birthday she had shown her mother proof of 'the curse' she had been told to expect for more than a year, and it was a week after its third return that her mother took her into the woods for a talk.

As they crossed the summit of the hill that separated their farm from the farm belonging to Esther's grandfather, her mother bent down and pulled off a piece of red thread wound around a rusted nail on a fence post. A little later, they went through a gate and into a cornfield, beside which she stopped to tear off a small branch from a cedar sapling that hung plush and low above the stones. She then stripped off the largest ear of corn she could find and put both items into the deep frayed pocket of her apron. She told her daughter about many other things she might have gathered on their walk, if their wishes for the future had been different. But as this was only a demonstration, they took the pieces home and waited for nightfall. It was autumn, and the heavy blue shadows from the forest fell early though the sky was lit in its southern half by the glow of the Hunter's Moon.

Taking Esther by the hand, mother taught daughter how to make a deep narrow V in the earth, into which she carefully spilled the kernels of corn, before putting in the cob, point downwards, the thread (which Esther learned had come from her father's shirt) and the evergreen branch. All of these charms she then carefully buried, telling Esther that if she had wanted the spell to work, she would have had to urinate on the spot to 'set the time'.

It was a night that Esther never forgot.

Six years later, when Esther first fell in love, she put to use some other knowledge, to which that evening had been a mere precursor. She, too, gathered things from her beloved's touch — bits of his clothing, soil left with the print of his shoes. With these she mixed other ingredients, like water from her well, strands of her hair, parings from her fingernails, and a drop of her blood. Most powerful of all was the symbol she posed for the gift of Jonas's love; a symbol that no one else could share and whose legacy would forever torment his dreams.

Ruth Ann was nine when the door into this world was opened for her. Esther took the girl to all the appropriate places, teaching her about the plants she would need, the signs she must read, the words she should speak. Ruth Ann listened attentively, without fear, but also without comprehension.

In two years, she seemed to have forgotten virtually everything her mother had said, and — worst of all — almost night by night, she had acted as tutor to Marcus. She taught him charms, instructed him in the use of 'cures', and even showed

him the hiding places around the house where their mother
kept her most private belongings. She did all of this confident
that Marcus's lacking in one essential would thwart his efforts
perpetually, and so tease him to failure.

But he forgot nothing. Season followed season and being naturally sensitive, he added together the things he had
learned with the things he observed all about him. To Marcus
it seemed no great wonder that the faded blue house, long-
shuttered by death, should once again live. Seeds fall, and
they grow, and they fall again. But what troubled him, what
drew him to this stranger, was that—like himself—Matteo
possessed a magic that he did not seem able to use, a gift
whose signs he had held in his hands almost from his birth,
but whose true promise slept inside him until the returning
spring charged once again the potency of the soil.

Matteo was asleep when Marcus found him. He had drawn
himself out full-length in the shade of the hillside facing the
valley, and white feathers of April sunlight floated upon his
face and arms. He slept with the abandon of one accustomed
to afternoon naps, and with the tangible delight of one returning to such ease after a long hard winter.

Marcus looked down on him from the height of the porch,
as astonished to find a grown man asleep while the sun was
still shining as he had been to hear one singing. He studied
the mouth that had formed the beautiful foreign words, as
it tricked up and down rhythmically with Matteo's breathing. Marcus was both glad and sorry to find Matteo sleeping.
Glad because he had never seen a man sleep outside, on purpose, and in the afternoon; sad because there were things he
wanted to talk about.

After ten minutes' wait, Matteo had still not awakened and

Marcus began to tap the heels of his boots against the porch wall. After five minutes more he gave up, pulling himself to his feet and looking about for some other way to pass the time.

The outside of the house seemed much more cheerful now, with two of its corners aglow with forsythia, and its front lane brightened with blossoming dogwood. The torn soil where he had helped Matteo dislodge many small stumps was now open once again to stripes of sunlight, and becoming overrun with a carpet of honeysuckle. Marcus walked softly across the cleared and freshly painted porch to find that Matteo had left his door open.

The house, silent in all of his memories of it, now held the low ticking of a clock—an heirloom that Matteo had proudly re-started after two decades of lifelessness.

Without really knowing why he did so, Marcus continued through the door and into the house. He was drawn on beyond the kitchen to a crescent of light that lay across the floor in the room where Matteo worked. What he saw when he entered the workroom brought a sudden hiccup to his throat.

All of the room's many shelves were crowded with toys. More shelves had been added above the windows and doorways, and the resplendent colours and shapes dazzled Marcus's eyes. The floor along three of the room's four walls was lined with boxes full of toys, and a rack above the work-scarred bench held many more half-finished pieces. Never before had Marcus seen such an abundance of wonder in a single place.

He lifted down one box and removed the lid, revealing numerous exquisitely formed and painted figures nestled inside. He reached into the box and carefully removed a single toy, turning it over and over in his fingers and marvelling at the colours. And yet his joy was fringed with apprehension; for nearly everywhere that Marcus saw a circle, that circle held the peculiar little eyes of the hex signs staring back at him.

Footsteps sounded on the porch, and Marcus replaced the toy and set the lid back on the box. After placing it quietly on the shelf, he went into the kitchen to say hello. A pile of daffodils and a dish of fresh mushrooms on the table distracted his gaze for a moment—just long enough for Matteo to see him across the glass of red wine he was pouring.

"Marcus! Hello! How are you? I didn't hear you come in."

The two of them looked at one another, each noting with surprise how the passage of just a few months can still leave changes on people's features.

"I was just looking. That's all."

"Looking at the toys?" Matteo laughed. "Yes, you must come and see them."

He pushed past the boy into the room, setting his glass on the bench and gesturing around. "You can play with them all. Which ones do you like best?"

Marcus, suddenly tongue-tied, looked around the room. His eye fell on the marionette laughing silently from the bench.

Matteo had reached behind one of the toy boxes for a large, flat board and knelt down to lay it out on the floor. "Have you ever seen one of these? It's a ... a ... well, what would it be in English?" He laughed. "I'm afraid I don't know."

Marcus examined the sloping board, studded with little brass nails and dotted with circles reading '10', '20' and '50'. Matteo pulled back a plunger and released its spring, sending a marble careering around its face.

Rather than watching the action of the game, Marcus kept his eyes fixed to the board's main decoration. Centred near its curved top was a large sprinkle of colours, plainly a magnified hex sign.

"Do you want to try your luck?" Matteo asked hopefully.

Startled, Marcus looked up at him.

"There sure seems to be more of them than there used to be."

"More of what?"

Marcus pointed to the top of the board.

"Oh?" Matteo hesitated. "I don't think so." His gaze swept the room, and his expression changed before Marcus's eyes. He stood up and put his hand on the boy's shoulder. "You're right."

Marcus smiled for the first time.

"Would you like a drink?" Matteo asked.

Marcus glanced towards the glass on the bench, where an unbroken bubble slept on the surface of Matteo's wine. "Sure" he said.

Marcus was engrossed in the board game by the time his host returned with a pink watery version of the wine. Matteo pointed to the painted sign. "What do you call this design again?"

Marcus hesitated, then whispered, "Hex signs."

"Oh. But you don't believe they're really magic?"

Marcus didn't answer. Matteo tried again. "Not like Ruth Ann believes."

"She don't know nothing."

"Do you believe in other magic?"

Marcus released the plunger and watched the marble trace a slow arc around the painted disc before dropping into a slot labelled '50'.

"No," he said, "except some things."

"What things?"

Marcus stood up and drew closer to Matteo's knee. "Well, when little babies has got the 'go backs' and looks like dying, there's people that can strip all their clothes off and can put a big circle o'red hot coals 'round them and read stuff out of the Bible and save them."

Encouraged by Matteo's attentive silence, Marcus went on,

"And old Puddly Dan, he could try for thrush and exzeema by making a little old triangle of straw on your tongue and a-saying stuff. Some people says that Ira can do it too by a-blowing through the straw and a-talking about Moses. When Dory's milk all went bad in the bucket, she put a broom across Reno's door and he up and nearly died of fever when he come out of the back of his house. Asa used to cut things in the milk to keep the witches off, but I don't know what it was. Then there's folks..."

Marcus stopped. Matteo, who had listened with polite attention to all of this, leant forward sympathetically. "Folks who... what?" he asked.

"Folks that can put 'hants' on ya," Marcus muttered.

"Oh," Matteo answered. "I suppose 'hants' are like hexes or spells or something?"

Marcus nodded.

"Who would do that?" Matteo asked.

Marcus looked up into Matteo's face. Seeing nothing but earnestness there, he whispered, "There's folks that says that your mama..."

"Marcus Farley!"

The shout came from outside, and belonged to Esther; Matteo and Marcus both looked down on her standing outside the room's closed window. Matteo crossed the room, and pushed open the window. As he did so, a wave of forest-cooled air pushed in. No longer as angry as she'd sounded, Esther grinned and shook her head.

"No, sir," she said, "never in all my born days have I seen two fellers that likes toys so much." In a moment she had gone around the house and joined them in the room. "Well, they sure are pretty, though."

She picked up a long narrow box, over which a smiling clown in a black hat somersaulted. Matteo sat down at his bench.

"This where all them trees went, then?" she asked.

Matteo smiled. "Some of them."

Having little faith in witchcraft and none in rumour, Matteo was not going to let the boy's gossip—or Esther's interruption of it—bother him. Although he knew the answer even before he asked the question, he offered Esther a drink.

"No, uh, I mean, no thank ya."

"But," he offered jokingly, "I have made a store of sarsaparilla with the sassafras that Marcus gathered for me in the autumn."

"No," she said, though a smile flickered across her face. "We best get a move on."

Marcus rose from where he'd been playing the board game, and all three of them went quietly back through the kitchen and outside. Instinctively putting his arm out in a gesture of embrace, Matteo lowered his hand to within a few inches of Esther's shoulder. "One evening, or perhaps on Sunday, you and Jonas, and the children might come around. I'd like to make you supper and hear more stories from these beautiful hills."

With a smile that said 'no,' she promised to ask Jonas when he came in for the night.

"I'd like the company," Matteo said, "and I love to hear about things, even when they're not true." Esther laughed a little at that. Encouraged, Matteo went on happily. "Yes, I do. I think Marcus was about to tell me that my father was haunted by witches."

Esther's smile vanished and Marcus's arm dropped just as he was about to throw a stone at a caterpillar.

"Um... um," she said, struggling to recover her smile. "What's that boy a mine been a-saying then? Your daddy got shot cause he scared a witch or something?"

Startled, Matteo drew back a step into the shadow of the new maple leaves over his head. "No...no. He only said..."

Before Matteo could finish, Esther threw back her head and laughed. "Shit! There ain't no mystery about it. Your daddy was shot cause he was a moonshiner, and that's all it is to it. Everybody knows that."

An icy-fingered pressure tightened around Matteo's temples. "A what?"

"Aw, you know. A moonshiner. He made corn whiskey and sold it. They're called moonshiners cause they work at night, by moonshine. It's against the law, but that don't matter. Hell, he wasn't the only one that did it. It'd a been better for him if he had a been."

A dark curtain fell over Matteo's mind. He felt again the taste of wine in his mouth, thinking of his mother's peculiar aversion to drink. "It's not true," he stammered.

Esther took Marcus by the hand, and spoke softly, more to her shoulder than to Matteo. "Well, I don't know. Maybe he was and maybe he wasn't, but it's what folks say."

Matteo stood there, stunned, and she took pity on him, resting her hand, calloused and white-lined from work, on his forearm. "It's nothing, really" she said. "If ya want to see for yourself, go on up there where you and them kids was a-looking for 'coons. I heard he used to have his still — that's the thing they cook it in — in there amongst all them apple trees, so as he could make applejack in the Fall. There might still be something to see."

With a supreme effort of self-control, Matteo thanked her, repeated his invitation to supper, and said goodbye.

For the rest of the afternoon and well past the time he liked to have his supper, Matteo sat silently on the porch swing looking out over the panoramic view. Below him he could see Jonas in a distant field, tenderly inspecting a tiny herd of young calves recently weaned from their mothers. From two directions came the sound of ploughing.

Matteo could hear the songs of blackbirds and smell the scent of freshly-turned earth, but felt only inertia brought on by a loss of direction. He had come to this place desiring above all things an emotional connection with the memory of his parents—to live as they had done in the place he knew they were happiest and to take that joy—only that joy—and make it his own; to drink it in like wine and allow it to become a part of his soul.

For the first time, Matteo could be honest: he had not come here on some vague whim; he had come with a purpose: vegetables would be grown as a pastime and not as a chore; toys would be created for the joy of it, trees would be cleared for the beauty yielded by the task.

He had groomed a life of comparative ease in a neighbourhood full of toil. And now, just when he wanted to feel that his work was finished and that he could rest, just as the business of contemplation seemed set to prosper, his spirit was tarnished by doubt.

He certainly did not want to look for the corroded remains of a 'moonshiner's still'. So what if his father made and sold liquor? Was that really any different from making and selling wine? Content with his memories of his mother, and mature enough to know that between couples some things are never agreed upon, he was no longer upset to think that it was so. What did it matter if one sold alcohol and the other didn't drink? Nonna had sipped marsala with a far greater relish than she showed for the best wine that Nonno ever made.

And yet the news troubled him, bringing disarray to the ordered instruments of his mind. It was as if he had found a forgotten photograph of someone he once loved, looking different from anything he thought possible.

Esther's words came back to him: 'He was shot because he

was a moonshiner.' His mother had told him that his father was killed by a man trying to steal something from him. She never said what it was the man was trying to steal, nor had that ever mattered to Matteo. Perhaps it was, after all, something to do with moonshine. What difference could that make now? There was no way to judge the past rightly on such grounds; if his father had done wrong, he forgave him.

Warmed with this forgiveness, Matteo thought that he might after all have a look at the place now associated in his mind with his father's memory. For months he had felt the presence of his parents' happiness in every floorboard, every joist, every room of their old home, and he had been pleased to enjoy the same sights that he knew they had enjoyed. To add something new to this collection was a pleasant thought, even if the feelings it brought were complex and not altogether harmonious.

He shouldered his axe and went into the woods towards the stream. In minutes, the low evening sun was lost in the darkness of the branches, through which he suddenly glimpsed the darting trajectory of a bat. He followed the course of the iron-coloured water uphill, pleased to see its swift bubbling between shoals of mossy stones. Unhurriedly, despite his growing hunger and the dimming light, he turned right from the stream and strolled through the woods, so eliminating a long and unnecessary journey along the creek he knew.

He flushed an enormous great-coated rabbit and watched as its bobbing white tail flickered over the bristling copper of last year's oak leaves. Soon, the look of the forest grew unfamiliar. Still certain that the stream was to his left, he pressed on, believing that the weird apple-tree hollow lay below a slight ridge just in front of him.

The fading light in the sky behind him soon illuminated a wide drift of white apple blossom. He stood under the low draping branches of the trees looking once more upon the cup-like depression of earth. Strangely, perhaps because of the failing light, the enclosure seemed smaller than before. He scuffed down the embankment, his feet turning over a furrow of soft black humus behind him.

He tried to recreate in his mind how the children had been arranged when Esther found them, though nothing seemed to match the blueprint of his memory. He had come into the hollow near its top end, so decided to walk downstream a bit, in the direction of his own house.

He had only taken a few steps when his foot slid along a wet board. He kicked aside the covering debris of dead leaves, revealing two rotted boards, nailed together into a long V-shape. A chain-like series of lumps in the leaf-mould suggested that more such boards lay decaying, running in a straight line at an angle to the stream. Matteo's pulse quickened. He decided to follow the line to see where it led.

The receding sun had dropped below the lowest branches, now, leaving the cup-shaped valley awash in a deep red-gold light. The line of boards came to an end, with nothing further to be seen. Matteo cast about the area, dragging his feet through the leaves. Suddenly, he felt something snag.

He stooped and lifted up a pair of iron hoops, possibly from a barrel that had long-since rotted. Several flat stones were gathered together into an open triangle, and a pile of wood sawn into lengths, worm eaten and littered with animal faeces, were the only other signs of human activity that remained.

In this little depression of the earth, watered by a small stream and within a halo of white blossoms, his father had spent nights brewing whiskey, to be sold illegally to his neighbours—something his mother would surely have deplored.

Putting such reflections aside, Matteo decided it was time to follow the sinking sun back home. A long detour seemed preferable to the prospect of picking his way through unfamiliar woodland in the darkness, so he kept to the stream-side. The last of the light clung to the uppermost branches and the woods in front of him grew blacker as he walked—and suddenly he was surrounded by another high curtain of apple trees.

He had not gone very far. He could barely make out the shape of the hollow, but what he saw was enough to tell him that this was the very place where he had looked for raccoons with the children.

Racing the encroaching darkness now, he quickly searched for signs of past work now lost in the leaves. With his hands and feet he felt over every lump that still showed, but nothing in the cold and crumbling dampness held a familiar shape. There was no sign of shelter, no visible axe marks on the trees, no evidence that anyone had ever used this spot for anything but apple-gathering. Plainly Esther had been wrong about some of her details.

With this thought, Matteo stood up and brushed the thick black earth off his hands. As he did so, the first gentle glow of silvered moonlight touched the treetops. Looking down at the light's reflection in the water, Matteo saw himself—a featureless, expressionless, unknowable dark shape of a man. Bending down to touch the water, he gingerly pushed aside a tangle of briar canes; the spangling noise of their movement almost drowned the sound of something dropping into the water.

Curious, he used his axe handle to prod the spot where the circles expanded in the shallow pool. As the wood touched bottom, branches on the other side of the stream jerked in time to Matteo's movements. He turned the axe around and used its head to hook out a long strand of wire from the water. Fragile with rust, it ran across the stream in both directions; as Matteo tugged it, a line of leaves lifted over the flat bed of the hollow, running away from the water.

He followed this line, twice kicking aside stones and once

having to pick up the loose end of the wire where time had eaten it through, until it reached a tall tree near the edge of the embankment. The wire ended at the tree, the bark having long since grown around the spot where it had been tied. As he looked up, he saw a forked pair of limbs, across which something lay.

The mixture of light from stars and moon was richer now and he could just make out a platform built from planks—now mostly broken up by the tree's growth—whose sawn ends were unmistakable.

Confused and growing colder, Matteo dropped the end of the wire and turned back in the direction of his own home.

Somewhere behind him a young owl called, but nothing in the deep silence of the forest answered back.

Chapter Eight

Grey fingers of cloud lay poised over the tree-tops when Matteo's screen door slammed shut behind him. The sand-like touch of a breeze — not yet completely free of the night's chill — pushed over his face and hair as he strode down the path towards Jonas's farm.

He was hurrying to see Marcus, hoping to catch up before the boy left for the cluster of ash trees where he awaited, each weekday morning, the uncertain arrival of the school bus.

Replaying the things he had experienced in the forest, alongside the echo of Esther's words, had left Matteo all but sleepless and spoiled his usual enjoyment of the first hours of morning. Despite his quick steps and straight course, he felt a bleary sense of misdirection.

He was also angry with himself for allowing his feelings to be so far drawn beyond his control. At a rational level, he knew exactly what had happened to provoke him: he had thought Esther mistaken, and now he wasn't sure. What was more, there was not one moonshine still, but two—one a little upstream of the place he had first visited. Nothing more deserved to be explained. And yet he was troubled.

The difference was that virtually everything he had encountered in his visit to his birthplace held some unique significance for him. His parents' home had been his own; the life they lived there, he had shared. The sights and sounds, stories, songs and dreams were all hung high on the hooks of his memory.

Random discoveries—like the words long-buried in the heart of the small tree—belonged to a distant past that was, nevertheless, his own. To discover the hidden and decaying things in the woods—forsaken or lost or misunderstood by the people who held some share in their meaning, and which had a tangible connection to the event that had changed his life forever— this was not gossip or hearsay; these things he could touch. Like the house, like the toys, these things were a part of the whole. Happiness alone was no longer enough to sustain him.

He was not at ease with what he knew about his father's death, but before the previous night he had been content that such things cannot be fully known, even though evidence might survive, even though people might remember. But the wood, the metal, even the apple-blossom that had clung to his hair with the falling dew, drew him onward to discover what it was that others truly knew.

Matteo was closing the gate to Jonas and Esther's dooryard when he heard the thunder of feet on stairs and the screeching of a door somewhere out of sight. Ruth Ann burst around the back of the house, running towards him. She held a brown and grey striped crock, and her face was contorted with disgust. She disappeared just beyond him, and he heard a splatching sound in the pig-pen, followed by several appreciative grunts. A moment later, she re-appeared carrying the empty crock at arm's-length.

She set the crock down on the path, and smiled. "Well, hi!"

The fumes from the vessel's interior reached Matteo's nose: a shocking, noxious reek of vinegar and herbal rot. He pulled a face.

Ruth Ann giggled. "Aw, don't mind that. It's just some of last year's kraut that stopped a-working. I gave it to the hogs. They'll eat anything."

"Is Marcus home?" he asked.

"No, he's done gone to school."

"Oh."

Ruth Ann's eyebrows drew together and Matteo realised he had been rude. He forced himself to smile. "And what about you, young lady? Why aren't you in school today?"

Inexplicably, the girl turned her back to him and muttered something about not being well, her hand passing lightly over her abdomen.

"Are your mother and father at home?" he asked.

"No," she said, still not turning around. "They're both out planting corn."

"So they've left the housework to you, have they?" he said lightly. "Can I help?"

Matteo knelt and picked up the foul-breathed crock. Ruth Ann watched as he carried it to the corner of the house where the old well stood. He placed the crock on the side of the stone square and seized the old steel pump handle, pistoning it up and down, expecting any moment that a gush of water would appear.

Ruth Ann ran towards him. "Hey, that don't work no more. Least I don't think it does."

She lay her hand on his as it rose and fell, and a low gurgle announced the arrival of a cascade of rust-coloured water. As she looked on, wide-eyed with surprise, he swung the crock underneath the rapidly-clearing flow, and soused the crock's insides, until they no longer stank.

He grinned at her. "Is there anything else I can do?"

She sparkled. "You want to help me?"

"I'd be happy to," he said. "If you'll let me."

He forgot all of his cares in the glow of appreciation that crossed Ruth Ann's face.

For more than an hour Matteo followed in Ruth Ann's wake. He helped her to empty a jar of dried beans into a pan for soaking; he carried two letters to the rusty mail box at the end of the farm lane; and he peeled the apples she needed to make dumplings. In all this time, she showed few outward signs of the illness that had prevented her going to school. Only once, as she stretched upward to put a clothes peg on the highest reaches of the line where she was hanging out sheets, did he notice her wince and once again lay her hands on her torso, below her stomach. Perhaps her illness was illusory or maybe she was feeling better as her state of mind improved with company.

When there no longer appeared to be anything left to do, Ruth Ann suggested that they have a cup of coffee. Matteo recalled with amusement the revulsion this drink had produced in the children the last time, but he did not dare to remind his hostess of this. Instead, he watched with fascination as she lifted down a large green jar from an overhead cupboard, unscrewed its zinc lid and spooned several measures into an immense coffee mill. She applied herself to the contraption's crank, and the mill settled down into a continuous crunching rumble. Then she paused to withdraw the drawer from the machine's base and proudly displayed its contents for Matteo's approval.

As the warm smell of the newly-ground coffee filled him Matteo was transported back to the last Saturday afternoon he spent with his grandparents before leaving the village to go to university.

His great-aunt Muretta had come all the way from town — ostensibly to see him before he left — although he really knew she had come to comfort Nonna, who was sure to weep at his leave-taking. With her, she had brought two of his cousins, neither one of whom he could remember ever having seen before. Antonio was nearly sixteen years old. He spoke little, was plainly full of himself, and easily distracted from the family circle by the passing-by of any woman under the age of fifty. The other cousin — Antonio's sister Lucinda — was a year or two older than Matteo. By day she worked in a secretarial capacity at a contractor's office — a fact of which Zia Murreta was extremely proud, twice drawing Matteo's attention to the fact that the two of them were examples of what the family could achieve.

Matteo remembered looking across the marble table at this young woman as the waiter set down a cup of coffee before her. She was wreathed in cigarette smoke — it seemed to twine itself with the looping curls of her hair and beyond the haze the colour of her eyes was a mystery. She was indeed fine-looking, though her studied determination to avoid looking at the others at her table left no doubt as to her high opinion of herself in relation to the company she was forced to keep that bright afternoon.

She was the sort of woman Matteo knew he could never love.

Disentangling his thoughts from the coffee's aroma, Matteo looked at Ruth Ann, whose eyes were on him through the steam of her cup.

"You haven't been to see me for a long time," he said.

She fidgeted. "Well, there's lots to do this time of year."

"Like what?"

Her eyes opened a little wider. "There's all kinds of things to plant: taters and beans and peas and I don't know what-all. There's stuff to fix, and everything to clean. I even got my own cow this year and when she has her calf, I'm going to rear it and keep the money when it's sold."

"Is that a good way to make money?"

"Aw, it's pretty good. Ain't a lot to do, except wait."

"What else do people do to make money?"

"There ain't much for a kid to do, except help with the hay and pick apples and all. There ain't even much for the grown-ups to do nowadays." She looked thoughtful for a moment. "Pap says that when his daddy was alive, there was all sorts of things a body could do."

"Like what?"

"Well, women used to get a spring wagon and go up into the woods and pick huckleberries to sell. They used to crack walnuts and make stuff like jelly and all. The men had all kinds of stuff they could do. They used to cut up the oak trees just to sell the bark for tanning hides, and they used the trees for ties on the train tracks. They used to use some kind of tree to make barrel staves during the war, but 'deed I don't know what kind they'd've been. There was stuff to trap for, like minks and muskrats and 'coons and all. And there was moonshiners and some fellers went up to the furnace to work in the mines and make iron."

She stopped and sipped at her coffee. As she was swallow-ing, Matteo thought about what she had said. Moonshining was a business like any other. A source of income for people who had few options.

He decided to try an experiment. "My father was a moon-shiner," he said.

Ruth Ann sat down her cup matter-of-factly and said, "That's right."

"But that was a long time ago."

She said nothing, so he continued. "Some people say that that's what killed him."

"No," she said, looking very serious, "I mean not directly. I just heard he got killed a-doing it."

"Doing what?"

"Well, what they used to do is to run water out of the crick through some kind of trough, and then into barrels full of corn, and when that corn was good and soggy and all, they'd cook it in a big copper thing with a pot on top like a funnel that'd catch the steam, and when the steam cooled down, it made the moonshine. Something like that. We learned about it in school."

"What was he doing when somebody shot him?"

"'Deed I don't know, but the thing is, they shouldn't have been able to get nowheres near him. That's what Sully says too."

"Why?" Matteo leaned forward, not wanting to miss a word. "What do you mean?"

"'Cause there ain't no moonshiner dumb enough to work by his self." She glanced at Matteo but he said nothing, and she continued, "They used to put at least one other feller up in the trees somewheres that they could see all 'round, so as if anybody was to come along they could warn the other feller, or sometimes shoot the one that was a-looking for them."

Matteo remained silent, thinking all this over and remembering the platform he had glimpsed in the trees near the stream.

"The thing is," Ruth Ann said, "whoever was supposed to be looking after him that night either didn't do his job right, or up and run off and left him; or they was in on it."

Matteo considered these options as Ruth Ann sipped her coffee and, with an almost imperceptible shudder, put the cup back on to the table.

"Ruthie? Ruthie?" Jonas's voice called from outside. Ruth

Ann got up to answer as her father's shadow appeared on the screen door. There was a momentary flash of astonishment on Jonas's features as he came into the room and saw the scene before him—two cups and saucers, pot of coffee, two chairs arranged to make conversation easy. Matteo stood up.

"Well How-do, old-timer!" Jonas boomed.

Matteo smiled weakly. "I hear you've been planting corn?"

Jonas laughed. *"Whool-wee,* we sure have been. Now I like to plant corn except for all them…" he paused, looked hard at Matteo, and mouthed the words 'god-damn,' "…little stones."

"Ruth Ann has made me some coffee," Matteo said. "I hope you don't mind."

"No! Hell no! I don't mind" he said, slouching into a chair. "You two just go on a-having tea parties. You keep it up and you'll civilise us yet. Hell, it's all I can do just to keep them in shoes."

Ruth Ann stomped her foot and put her hands on her hips. "That ain't true!"

Jonas's answer was a laugh.

"Matthew's been a-helping me do my chores," she said, "and they're all done now."

"Uh-huh" her father replied. "You want me to think of some more?"

Ruth Ann folded her arms and sat down.

"Now, you just go on and get my dinner in there directly, girl, ya hear? Your mama's gone down to your Pap's to take him some of them mushrooms you and Marcus found, and she'll get something there."

"Oh," Ruth Ann muttered as she got up and began to lay the table.

Jonas shook his head. "You alright up there?" he said to Matteo. "Ain't seen you 'round much at all."

"I've had a lot to keep me busy," he said, trying to keep his voice light despite his preoccupation with Ruth Ann's revelations.

Jonas rubbed his hands together. "Yes, sir, I expect you been as busy as the button on an outhouse door." He paused. "You got all ya need, or come a-looking for something? I mean if I got something ya need, don't bother with asking, just take it and bring it back when you're done. That's alright. Sorry Esther ain't here to say how-do."

Touched by his neighbour's kindness, Matteo relaxed. "No," he said, "I'm alright. I just came down to say hello, and have a talk with Marcus about the place where we looked for racoons. Ruth Ann said he had already left for school, so I stayed to help her because she said she wasn't feeling very well."

Jonas leaned forward and whispered so that Ruth Ann, who was taking a pie down from an overhead cupboard, wouldn't hear. "That's real good of ya and all, but it ain't nothing. Just female troubles, you know."

Matteo nodded, and Jonas perked up as Ruth Ann came back to the table with a loaf of bread.

"So where'd Sully take ya looking for 'coons then? This side of the mountain, or over by Huntin' Crick?"

As nonchalantly as possible, Matteo said, "Upstream, where my father's still used to be."

Jonas stared into space for a moment, and his burly brows drew slowly together. He twice began to speak, but trailed off. In the end he simply nodded and said, "Oh."

"That's right, Daddy," Ruth Ann said. "We was just talking about how Sully and me figures it was his daddy's lookout's fault that his daddy got shot."

Jonas's grin pulled itself a little sideways, and he stood up. Then he sat down again. "No, now don't you be speculating about things that happened before you was born." He picked up a spoon, set it down again, picked it up once more, set it down, then carefully lined it up with the woodgrain of the tabletop. "Say, Ruthie, you give Matthew back that thing that you and Marcus took from him last time you was up there?"

"I didn't take nothing. Sully took it."

"Well, I don't care who took it, you just give it back, ya hear?"

"I don't know where it is. Sully put it somewheres so as I couldn't get it."

"Well, you just go and find it then, a'for ya forget."

Ruth Ann set a large blue-patterned charger filled with slab-like pieces of cold ham on the table, and left the room.

Matteo could hear her bare feet slapping the treads of the stairs. "Was it a toy?" he asked.

"Aw, I don't know. Esther said it was some kind a little 'coon or something. Say..." Jonas said, in the same bright tone with which he had spoken to Ruth Ann, "don't you pay no attention to what them kids tell ya. They hears shit and get it all mixed up. Your daddy's shooting didn't have nothing to do with no lookout." Jonas paused, then once more busied himself with aligning the cutlery. "I mean it did, I guess. But them fellers what got him would of got him sooner or later anyway."

"What fellows?"

Jonas pushed his chair back from the table and stood up. Not looking at Matteo, he walked across the room to the sink and started to wash his hands. "Aw, I don't know exactly. Ain't nobody knows for sure." Jonas's voice was loud over the roar of water from the kitchen tap. "Everybody says it was some of them Hessins that live further up the mountain, right at the top nearly in Pennsylvania, something they was in on. Shit, they're all so backwards up there, could be any of them that might of shot him in broad daylight, let alone at night." He turned off the tap and reached for a tea towel.

"Why would they have shot him?" Matteo asked in a near-whisper.

Jonas returned to the table and sat down across from Matteo. "Well," he said, "they was moonshiners too. But it wasn't them that shot him. No, sir." He leaned down, almost crouching in his chair and speaking in a low voice. "I don't remember much about it, 'cause I was still little at the time and folks likes to keep such stuff away from young ones, ya know, so as I didn't hear much about it till I was older and my mama told me. What she said is that some of them folks come along one night and put kerosene in the crick up above there where his still was on the night that he was a-working. He didn't know nothing about it, see, and the story goes that some of that whiskey he sold up and killed one feller, and it was his people that come along and shot him. Esther's daddy'll tell ya that it might've even been the feller's widow, 'cause he said he could hear a woman a-screaming up in them woods. But I don't know."

Matteo was spellbound. Here at last was the story of what had happened: rival moonshiners; a poisoned water supply; a dead customer. The victim's family would have had no other redress, because the business of buying and selling moonshine was illegal, so they took the only vengeance they could on the man they thought responsible. Matteo's mother would have also been powerless, because her husband had been murdered while committing a crime himself. So.

Matteo felt angry and frustrated, but at least the story made sense.

He looked at Jonas, who sat with his eyes very wide open and his head low, as though he could read the past in the vacant cream space of the kitchen floor. Matteo sensed no evidence of pretence or evasion on Jonas's part, and it had been related like a story that Jonas knew well. Probably others did too. The shame that had been present in his voice as he spoke touched Matteo to the heart. This man was a good neighbour and Matteo trusted him as a friend.

"Thank you for telling me."

Jonas looked surprised. "Aw, it ain't nothing except what everybody knows. Shit, there's a lot that goes on in these hills; or least there used to be. It's all a'changin' now."

He had more to say, but Matteo was no longer listening. Hearing the rummaging upstairs, he stood up to go, laying his hand on Jonas's shoulder as he did so. "Do you need any help with that corn you're planting?"

"No, sir-ee," Jonas answered quickly. "We're alright. If the sun keeps a-shining like this, and Marcus'll help me in the evenings. But thank ya and all."

A lingering sadness on the older man's face prompted Matteo to repeat his invitation for Jonas and Esther to come to his house for supper. Pleased but anxious, Jonas accepted, promising to visit as soon as the corn was planted.

Matteo closed the screened door behind him as he left, and faced the full breadth of the midday sun as he set off for home. The air held a scent like perfume and fruit, and the southwest breeze drifted over the cherry-blossoms fringing the hay fields beyond Jonas's house.

Looking out across the stone-framed fields, Matteo saw the distant figure of a woman moving towards the house. It must be Esther, he thought, hurrying home to another afternoon's work.

With a renewed spring in his step, Matteo rubbed his hands together, trying to rid himself of the strangeness of being out for a walk without the familiar weight of his axe. The pool of his thoughts grew still and calm. With nothing to disturb him, he decided to pick up the axe and then drift off for a ramble in the forest.

As he hopped across the stones in the stream below his house, he heard a voice cry out: "Matthew!"

He turned and saw Ruth Ann, pale and puffing and just beginning to sweat. "Well, sir," she said, "you sure can walk fast when you want to. Didn't you hear me calling ya all that way?"

"No, I'm sorry. I was thinking. Is anything the matter?"

"No. It's just that Daddy wanted me to give this back to ya before ya left, but you'd done went off before I could catch ya."

"What is it?"

The girl held out her open hand, and Matteo stretched his own hand towards her. Just as their fingers met mid-way across the stream, whatever it was slipped out of her grasp and fell into the water with a small fillip. Both knelt down, and Matteo was the first to see it. Resting on the gravelly bed beneath the water was the small wooden racoon that had transfixed Marcus's attention. Matteo retrieved it and held it up for the sun to dry.

"It's a racoon" he said.

"Sure is."

Matteo laughed. "Tell your mother I found a racoon in the stream after all."

Ruth Ann turned away and walked back towards her own house, leaving Matteo altogether alone.

Chapter Nine

Kneeling down with his face only a few inches from the ground, Matteo carefully dug out the spiralling tendrils of weeds that had rooted amongst the crowns of the autumn-planted artichokes. In spite of their long journey and the hard winter cold, the plants were faring well and the new shoots were already more than a foot tall.

Running his fingers over the prickly leaves, he looked up into the vast uncluttered sky, straightened his back and began to sing. The song peaked and fell as he moved from plant to plant, and his voice travelled far over the quiet fields and into the empty woods. In harsh counterpoint to his singing, he could hear a pair of sparrows perched in the trees at the end of the rows, loudly and intermittently disputing their territorial rights.

When the last plant was weeded, he clapped the loose soil from his hands, stood up and turned around to admire the progress he had made. Near the place where he had started crouched Marcus, who was examining one of the plants sceptically.

"Good morning, Marcus! 'Long time, no see' — that's the phrase isn't it?"

"What you going to do with all them thistles?" the boy said without looking up.

"Eat them."

Matteo's answer got the effect he desired. Marcus stared at him, open-mouthed and Matteo laughed out loud.

Marcus closed his mouth and shook his head. "Unh, unh," he said.

"They're not really thistles," Matteo said. "They're artichokes. Like thistles, but you can eat the flower bud before it opens."

Marcus looked a little relieved, but still incredulous.

"They call them that 'cause they choke ya?"

Matteo laughed. "Not the way I prepare them."

Marcus gathered up some stray weeds and set them on the pile Matteo had started, then sat down in the shade of a locust tree, where the sparrows once again remonstrated. "Ruth Ann said you was a-looking for me last week" he said.

"That's right. Nothing important. I was only going to ask you more about the racoons."

At the word 'racoon,' Marcus's eyes grew round and he looked away.

Matteo carried on with his weeding, passing from shoot to shoot of green garlic. "But it's alright now," he continued. "Your sister's told me all I wanted to know."

"She don't know nothing," the boy bristled.

"I only wanted to know whether there are other places like the one we visited with the apple trees."

"'Course there are. Lots of 'em. 'Specially up the mountain there towards the state line."

"Are there any more on the same stream we looked at?"

"Yes, sir-ee, there's one more, just up the crick a-ways."

With a sudden rush of apprehension, Matteo realised this was already going further and faster than he wanted it to. Today was Saturday. For five days he had been content with the things he had been told by Ruth Ann and Jonas. Now, once more, he felt the bridge shaking under him. "Then there were two stills?" Matteo asked.

"Yep. But the one's all gone, and ain't nothing left of the other 'cept some boards and all."

"But the place we saw together—that one was my father's?"

"No, sir, that was your granddaddy's before he give it up. The other one was your daddy's."

Matteo stopped working.

"My father's was the one upstream?" he asked.

"That's what Pap says."

"But why did my grandfather give up his still?"

"'Deed, I don't know."

"Were both stills working at the same time?"

Marcus shrugged. "I just don't know. Ya ought to talk to Pap about it. He knows all about them places in the old days."

Matteo thought for a moment. 'Pap' must be Marcus's grandfather—Esther's father.

"Where does he live?" Matteo heard himself asking.

"Who?"

"Your 'Pap'".

"Why? You want to talk about it?" Marcus jumped to his feet. "I could take ya, then I could maybe show ya the places he tells ya about."

Matteo looked at his half-weeded garlic. It was nearing midmorning and the sun was blazing. Perhaps a respite would do him some good.

"Can I?" Marcus persisted.

"Alright."

Matteo and Marcus went side-by-side down the stony lane from Matteo's house, towards the road. Watching their twinned shadows moving before them, Matteo reflected how his own father would have seen a similar sight, once, as he walked beside his son.

Instead of following the road, Marcus climbed up on a pile of stones, widened the gap between two strands of barbed wire, and gestured for Matteo to follow him into the field beyond. They went on for a short distance in a direction Matteo had never taken. From the crest of a small hill, Marcus pointed down to a cluster of trees and buildings at a junction where two roads met a stream. Matteo recognised it instantly as the place where he had asked directions the first day he arrived.

"He'll be down there this morning," Marcus said.

Twenty minutes later, the two of them had covered the distance that had taken Matteo an hour by road.

As they neared the porch step, Matteo heard the thin hum of the Coca-Cola machine compressor and glanced at the empty chair next to it.

The shop appeared deserted and to Matteo's surprise, that left him feeling a little relieved. It was because the old man might have had company, he decided. He didn't want to face a group of Ephraim's friends.

"Hi Pap!" Marcus shouted into the void.

Matteo turned around in time to see Marcus disappearing behind the counter and run clatteringly up some stairs. He heard the rumble of voices, and a chair slid back on the floor above his head. A moment later, and he was looking into the same flaring eyes of the old man who had been the first to meet him on his return.

"Well, I'll be damn!"

"Hello," Matteo stammered. "I…"

"Ephraim. I'm Ephraim. And I know all about you."

"Pap," Marcus said, "Matthew and me wants to know about stills and all and who use to own what, and I don't know what-all. I figured you would know pretty near everything."

A shadow flickered over Ephraim's face.

Embarrassed, Matteo recalled his own words the first time the two of them met, and he felt the old man's gaze run over his features. Then the old man threw back his head and laughed.

"*Who-who-wee!* So you and Matthew wants to know, do ya? You're just old friends now, I expect?"

Still smiling, Ephraim shuffled past them and out of the door. Through the window, Matteo saw him carefully lowering himself into his battered chair.

Marcus grinned, slapped Matteo on the arm and ran outside. The slamming of the screened door behind him seemed to knock a hole in Matteo's resolution. He now had to choose between swallowing his pride and listening to Ephraim's tale or finding an excuse to claim that the whole thing was a misunderstanding. Hearing the other two chatting, he went to the door and stepped onto the porch.

Matteo's composure returned as he passed by Ephraim's chair. He leant against one of the roof posts, one foot on the step, his face turned away towards the fields. "I can't stay long," he said softly. "Marcus is the curious one. He brought me here to see you today. I know all I need to know."

He turned back to the others. Ephraim had slouched down in his chair, lying nearly flat with his chin propped against his chest, pushing out the rounded sweaty jowls around his face. His words came in a low rumbling growl. "This boy says that Ruth Ann told him that their daddy done told ya that the whole thing blew up over some poison moonshine. Poison, my hind leg. That whole story's a crock of shit."

The back of Matteo's neck prickled with apprehension. "Why is that?"

"'Cause your daddy's still was the one uphill from the other one, that's why. If somebody had put something in the water up there, then it would've poisoned them both, and it didn't."

"How do you know?"

Ephraim's face flushed a bit. "'Cause I do, that's how."

"So who did my grandfather give the other still to?"

Ephraim laughed again. "Shee-ut! He didn't give it to nobody, and he didn't sell it neither. He just lost it."

"How did he 'lose' it?"

Ephraim sat up straight again, and the egg-shaped bulge of his belly sagged between his knees. The motion made his trouser hems ride up, revealing the pale skin above his white socks.

"Well, sir," he said, "your granddaddy was a happy man and always had a laugh about him. Your daddy, old George, was a happy man too. Always a-laughin' and a-cuttin' up. I expect you're a happy one too, if ya knew it. Anyways, your daddy weren't the only one that besides you made toys, 'cause your granddaddy did too. Well, one day when Pa—that's my Pa—kept store here, your granddaddy come down on a Sunday like the other fellers, and he brought with him one of them gizmos of his, and the fellers all started to take the shit out of him on account of his making these things and all. So he up and says that he's the luckiest feller in the whole Run—that's these here woods 'round here—and that he could prove it. So he takes this thing of his and plays Put-and-Take with them all, and beats them too. Then up steps a feller and says, 'Hey, I'll bet ya all that piece of ground there up the crick from your house that I'm luckier than you.' Well, the boys all went to town a-laughing, 'cause they knowed he meant the still and all. Then your granddaddy up and laughs too, and they played another one, and he lost. Shit, he didn't even care. But the boys all said that the feller that won ought to least-ways give him the apples off the trees so as that he could have something to cook next Fall. That's how he lost it."

Interested, and a little relieved, Matteo asked, "Who did he lose it to?"

Ephraim jerked his head in Marcus's direction. "This one's other granddaddy."

"You mean Jonas's father?"

"Yep."

"Was he a moonshiner too, then?"

Ephraim said nothing, but his face reddened slightly as he gazed into the distance behind Matteo's head. After a pause, he met Matteo's eyes and inclined his head in an almost imperceptible nod.

Then he whispered, "He…quit just after your daddy died."

"Why?"

Ephraim shrugged. "Don't know. 'Course the story 'bout the poison moonshine got 'round, and folks just reckoned he didn't want to take no chances."

"What happened to them stills, Pap?" Marcus asked.

Ephraim shifted his weight uncomfortably. "Well, the one that was George's just got away, I guess. Folks took it and sold the copper and all, and left the rest to rot, I reckon. I helped your daddy—'cause he was still a boy and all—to tear down the other one that was his daddy's, cause he didn't want no signs of it on his land no more."

Matteo tried to ground himself, pressing his back against the porch post's sharp corner, but his thoughts were adrift in a polluted darkness. He felt himself becoming the child he had once been, before he'd accepted that his mother's offering of uncertainty and confusion was all he should ever trust. Now, the terrible weight of not knowing pressed on him again. How could his father, the 'happy man' of his neighbours' memory, have become involved in such things?

Matteo smiled bitterly at Ephraim. "You missed some."

"Huh?"

"Some wire, running around on the ground. And some boards up in a tree."

"Oh, that." The old man looked relieved. "That wasn't part of the one we took down. That was from the first one, the one that belonged to George. Jonas said we wasn't to touch nothing that his daddy didn't put there."

"Them wires was for protection," Marcus said. "Fellers use to run them all 'round the woods, then if somebody come along in the dark they'd run into them and make a noise so that the feller up in the trees could hear them and warn the other one." He paused. "Or shoot them," he added softly. "That's why me and Ruth Ann figures the lookout weren't no dern good."

Ephraim stood up and leaned against the other porch post, rubbing up and down like a hog with an itch. Matteo watched him from the corner of his eye. The old-timer was staring at the dense blue forest that cloaked the mountains.

"Who do you think shot him?" Matteo asked quietly.

Ephraim scuffed his feet and spat into the grass below the porch. "I'll tell ya today what I told everybody else that's ever asked me that: I sure as hell don't know, and I don't think there's any goddamn way of finding out."

Nodding his head and letting the cool unhappy smile harden around his lips, Matteo dropped some coins into the Coke machine and pulled out a bottle. He opened it, then dug two cents from his pocket and pressed them into Ephraim's hand.

He then turned his back on the store and walked away, heading homewards again across the fields.

"Wait up! Wait for me, will ya! Matthew!"

It was Marcus. Matteo paused at the edge of a stand of new-ly-planted corn, the small green shoots combing the earth and the infant leaves waving in the breeze. He looked back at the boy, who was running to catch up. Then he turned away and went on more slowly.

Marcus caught up in a few moments, then fell into step alongside, breathing heavily. Just beyond the summit of the hill, Matteo stopped. Spread out before him was the moun-tainside on which he and many of his ancestors had lived. His own house nestled amidst the trees on the right, and below it and to the left stood Jonas and Esther's home. He had never seen them from this angle, and the unexpected beauty of it all—robed in gorgeous spring sunlight—made him catch his breath.

"Guess he don't know everything," Marcus said at last.

"Who?" Matteo answered distractedly.

"Pap."

"No, I didn't think he would."

"Ya want to see one of my favourite spots?"

"No, I must be getting back."

"It ain't far."

"No, thank you."

"It's just 'round there," Marcus said, pointing to the left. "Aw, c'mon, it's just there, I promise. I got something Pap don't know about."

Matteo looked at him.

"Something I found up there that he and Daddy didn't get. C'mon, Matthew." He set off towards the left.

With a sigh, Matteo followed Marcus to a point just around the top of the hill, and onward to where a pile of rocks lay atop a huge boulder.

As Marcus scrambled in front, Matteo could see why the boy had chosen this place; though it looked very rugged it was sheltered from the wind. The view of the countryside was even better here.

He sat on a stone near the top, and watched Marcus levering up a large flat rock near the base, revealing a small hole. Marcus reached inside and carefully withdrew a dried turtle shell, an empty Jack Daniels bottle, a silver cap gun missing its hammer, and a wooden cigar box. He replaced everything else, but brought the cigar box up to the rock and sat beside Matteo.

"Now you got to promise me that ya ain't going to tell nobody what I got. Okay?"

Amused but impatient to be gone, Matteo promised.

Marcus put the box on his knee, opened it and removed some folded sheets of glossy magazine paper that he weighted with a stone. Under the edge of the stone, Matteo recognised a naked breast.

Marcus then laid aside several other items, including a pocket watch that was missing its crystal, a beer bottle opener and a rusted penknife with a broken point. Then, looking straight at Matteo's face, he took out a long beaded chain.

"It's a necklace," he said, holding it up in the light.

Matteo studied it carefully. It was an ancient string of grey-black beads, separated at regular intervals by tiny silver birds, and ending in a loop from which hung a silver oval and a cross.

He looked at Marcus and smiled. "That's not a necklace," he said. "It's a rosary."

The boy looked disappointed. "A...what?" he said.

"A special thing that people — Roman Catholic people — use to help remember their prayers. It's called a rosary." Matteo put out his hand and took it into his grasp.

Running his fingers over the beads — chilly to the touch

from having lain so long under the stones — he showed Marcus how the chain was used. The boy's face glowed with interest.

"...and that's what it's for," Matteo finished. He held the string up towards the sun, spreading the rosary out into a wide circle with his fingers, and letting the yellow sunlight fall through it onto his face. Blinking, he focussed on the back of the silver oval joining the main circle with the pendant string. Engraved there were the letters, 'L.A.R.' He cupped the beads into his hands. The initials had been his mother's.

"Where did you find this?" he asked quietly.

"Up there in the woods."

Matteo leaned closer. "Where exactly?"

"Near where them stills was. Up in the trees. On top of them old boards that you must've found your own self the other day."

"Did you find anything else there?"

"Naw, the whole thing was covered in squirrel shit and I don't know what-all."

Matteo looked at the rosary and recalled the olive pit that he had spat out on his first day — 'the only one for fifty miles.' He glanced at the boy and then looked away, giving himself time for unjustified anger to subside into pity. He did not want to frighten Marcus, who didn't even know what he had found; the initials were meaningless to him. What else should he have done except hide it in a hole inside a box with other keepsakes? Matteo laid his hand on Marcus's shoulder.

"This was my mother's," he said, pointing to the initials. Then gauging the confusion on Marcus's face, he explained, "Her last name was Richetti before she married my father."

Marcus nodded, a little sadly. "I guess if that was your mama's then it ought to be yours now."

Matteo was caught between pain and indecision. Almost certainly, it was his mother's rosary. How it came to be on the platform would, he suspected, remain a mystery. Perhaps it had been stolen, perhaps thrown there, perhaps even a squirrel or bird had carried it into the trees. He would never know.

He forced himself to recall the days of his mother's decline, when she sat on the iron chair looking out towards the forest and terraces that lay beyond Nonno's house. He remembered that in her hands she sometimes held a rosary — a larger one than this — made of irregular dark wooden beads. It occurred to him at that moment that perhaps the second rosary had been fashioned by his father. The cold weight of the beads in his hands pulled him back to the present. He looked at Marcus.

"You can keep it if you want to," he said. "You're the one who found it."

"Naw," the boy answered. "That wouldn't be right. Besides, I can't show it to nobody anyhow."

"Why?"

"'Cause they'd all just want to take it away for their own selves." He stood up and took a couple of steps forward. "I'd like it better if you kept it." He looked at Matteo, squinting into the bright sun.

"Alright." Matteo slipped the rosary into his shirt pocket. "You know, some people like to carry them around because they think they're good luck. It's strange, isn't it, how something that's supposed to be a tool to help people talk to God, can be treated like … as if it were magic."

Marcus knelt down to replace the covering over his hoard.

"Do you believe in God?" Matteo asked.

"Yeah."

"Do you think He allows such things to help people?"

"I don't know. But I know He does stuff his own self."

"Like what?"

"Protects folks and all"

"How does He do that?"

"Makes them lucky themselves. Like you."

Matteo smiled. "Me? Why me?"

"Well, up there 'round your house is the lar trees, and they was all there before you got there, and I reckon that long as you stay up there in amongst them, ain't nothing bad could happen to ya."

"Why?"

"'Cause I don't know but I expect that them lar trees is good luck and you got three of them 'round your house. It's only God could've put ya in there."

Matteo found himself comforted by Marcus's curious blend of folklore and faith—a God who protects those he loves by putting them near lucky trees—and he felt himself relaxing into a gentler mood.

Content once again that the enigma of these people and this place where insuperable, and resigned to the haphazard way he would have to re-fashion his own relationship with them both, he stood up and patted Marcus on the back.

"Come on," he said. "Walk home with me. We'll have a bite to eat, and I'll show you the latest things I've made."

When they reached Matteo's doorstep, Marcus went in first, as if it had been his own home. He took down the plates and knives and laid the table without being asked. When the meal was over, he carried the crockery to the sink for washing-up. As Matteo tidied, Marcus went outside to the porch swing. The creaking sound of its rusted chains brought Esther's words back to Matteo—*time to settle down, have children, feather his nest*. It was pleasant having Marcus and Ruth Ann and the others about. They were earnest, full of surprises, and naively conniving in a way that charmed and appalled him by turns.

The knowledge, when it came, hit him like a sudden splash of icy water: one day soon, Matteo would have to decide where to spend the rest of his life.

He put down the last of the washing-up, dried his hands, and went into his workroom, both to steady himself and to see what he thought Marcus would enjoy most as a present. The boy had been generous about the rosary beads, and Matteo planned to honour the gesture in equal measure.

He looked around the shelves and boxes at the brightly painted toys, many of them now dusty from disuse. On his workbench lay a half-finished spinning top, its square sides tapering down to a point, directly above which — in the centre of a carefully executed hex sign — was the hole he had drilled for the spindle. He had owned a top like this when he was a boy, though it had been lost long ago. He had stopped work on the toy because he couldn't recall exactly what had decorated the top's four square sides.

Forgetting his initial motive, and hoping that perhaps Marcus might have seen something similar, Matteo decided to take it, along with the still unfitted spindle, outside to ask his opinion.

"Marcus," he called as he approached the outside door. "Have you ever seen one of these?"

Marcus stopped swinging and took the two pieces of wood in his hands. "It's a top," he said. "Some kind of top."

Unable to spin it because of the unattached spindle, he sat tracing the hex sign with his fingers. That gave Matteo an idea. "I haven't quite finished it yet." He touched the spindle. "This piece still needs to be fastened, and I can't decide what to put around the sides."

Marcus turned it over and over, then looked blankly at Matteo.

"I was going to ask you to help me but, I'll tell you what: I'll give it to you like this, and you can finish it any way you like."

Marcus was silent.

Matteo seated himself on the swing next to him. He then

pushed his feet gently against the porch floor to start the swing rocking.

Marcus looked up. "You sure I can keep it?"

"I'm sure." Matteo glanced at the boy. The small smile on Marcus's face shone alternately in light and shadow as they continued to rock the swing.

Chapter Ten

A mist the colour of powdered ginger wreathed the mountainside, dissipating in the brightness of a spring morning that already dreamed of summer, lingering in the wooded hollows worn smooth by the streams. Somewhere, in distant villages that Matteo had never seen, church bells rang faintly.

As he crouched to manoeuvre himself between the two strands of barbed wire by the roadside, he could already hear the soft clucking noise of laughter from the cluster of ash trees behind Ephraim's shop.

He went around the corner of the building. Seven strangers were standing about with their hands in their pockets, talking. Five of the men were dressed in dungarees; the other two wore canvas trousers with long sleeve shirts that opened at the neck in wide, hairy Vs. Each wore a hat, which in Matteo's eyes were either pulled down too far over the eyes, or pushed back too far off the forehead.

He smiled in the friendliest way he knew. "Morning," he said, burying his hands in his own pockets.

He was answered with a chorus of 'How-do,' 'Howdy,' and 'Morn.'

The tallest of the men turned to his ancient, cigar-smoking neighbour. "Anyhow, it ain't."

The older man's stogie glowed red, and he withdrew it from his mouth and examined it, exhaling a wide cloud of Virginia tobacco. Brown leathery wrinkles disappeared up under his hat brim as he raised his eyebrows. "You don't know shit."

"Ain't nobody going to tell me that there's something better than one of Fanny's applesauce cakes with black walnuts in it."

"I done told ya, you don't know shit," the older man said. "And that proves it."

"Aw, them people of yours would've lived on acorns if they'd a-had any teeth to chew 'em."

The old man executed a perfect smoke ring, clamped the cigar between his teeth again, and muttered sideways, "Shee-ut."

"Hey," the smallest of the men said, "ever been up there to the Lord's Acre? Hell, them girls *can* cook. *Whool-wee!* I bought a shell-bark cake up there with some of that honey on top … Umm-mmm, now that's eatin'."

As the men had been speaking, their irregular circle had begun—with gradual feet-scuffing—to widen, issuing to Matteo an unspoken invitation to join the group.

The man to his left—mid-thirties, blonde hair, red beard and smelling like a well-cleaned barn—leant towards him and spoke quietly. "You're getting that place of yours all fixed up?"

Matteo nodded. "It takes a long time."

"Sure does." The man sighed. "Sure as Hell does."

"I hear you got a good axe," the tall man said.

"*You* got a good axe," the old man answered. "*He* just knows how to swing it. *You*," he said — pointing his cigar to the bigger one's chest — "you couldn't hit a barn with a shovel."

"Shit on you."

The old man turned to Matteo and said, "That place still got all them rocks 'round it?"

Matteo laughed. "It's got too many rocks."

"Hell, Dorsey," the red-bearded man said to the cigar-smoker, "we all got too many rocks. Daddy use to say that they was a present from the Injuns."

"That and tobacco," the tall man said. "But at least tobacco kills some folks. Rocks just makes you wish you was dead."

The men chuckled, all except old Dorsey, who looked at the tall man and grinned without removing his cigar. "Gaither," he said, "you come 'round some time when I got a rock in my hand and I'll show what it can do."

This was answered with hoots of laughter, until Dorsey took the stogie out of his mouth and used it to point to Matteo.

"Only I was wondering," he said, "if you might be a-thinking of renting or selling them fields and all."

Before he had heard the words actually spoken to him, this idea had never even crossed Matteo's mind. He could feel the eyes of everyone present waiting for his answer, and he knew that his hesitating would be misinterpreted. A reasonable man himself, it was reasonable to him to suppose that these men would be interested in land that had once been cultivated, and that was now of no use to its owner. He could not let himself be deaf to such a proposal. And yet the unexpectedness of being asked combined with an uneasiness that he couldn't explain.

"What you want them for, Dorse? Ain't you got enough acres to work as it is?" a voice called.

All the men looked up, and Matteo turned around, as Jonas strode towards the group.

"Well, how-do, stranger," Gaither said. "What you doin' here? How come that woman of yours ain't got ya there in church then, like always?"

Jonas looked towards him with a scowl, but before he could reply the red-bearded man broke in happily. "Maybe she don't know he ain't there yet."

"She'll be down here looking for ya, I'll tell you what," another man said.

"Shit on it," Jonas answered.

Knowing that his friend really was a regular church-goer, and much surprised at his ill-temper, Matteo stood closer to him. He guessed how little Jonas liked to be teased about relations with his wife, so he spoke up, trying to deflect attention from Esther and back to the previous topic.

"No, sir," he said to Dorsey. "I couldn't think of doing anything like that without asking Jonas's advice. When I first came here...came back here... it was Jonas who showed me around and helped me to get settled in. Without him, I wouldn't even know which fields are mine."

Matteo glanced at Jonas. To his surprise, his friend's face was darkened with unfamiliar anger. Before he turned away, he caught the whiff of alcohol on Jonas's breath.

"Oh, yeah," muttered a fat oval-faced man. "He knows all about them fields, I expect."

"What's that mean?" Jonas growled.

The red-bearded man joined in. "Well, nothing, except that you lived up 'round there all your life, and all your people too."

"Uh-huh," Jonas answered. "Didn't hear nobody ask you nothing about it, Rube." He turned to Matteo with a bitter smile. "Anyway, I can see that you got all kinds of friends now. Or maybe you don't know them too good yet? This one here," and he pointed to the bearded man, "is called Rube. His real name's Seymour, but since his beard started to grow folks has said he looks like a ruby. He lives up that hill at a farm called Good Hope. Now this here's Gaither, and Dorsey, and them two over there looking like bumps on a log is called Ira and Asa."

Matteo glanced towards the two men Jonas had indicated. Neither would meet his eyes; both seemed distinctly uncomfortable with Jonas's introduction.

"They're twins, except they don't look the same." Jonas continued. "Folks said that was 'cause they had two different daddies. Their place is 'round that a-way and it's called Phillip's Delight." Wheeling about, Jonas looked at the others. "Then there's Herschel here, and that's Hobart—Hobart Plunkett that smells like a skunkett."

Before anyone could answer, Ephraim's voice thundered from the corner of the store porch. "Je-sus Chri-ust!" He slammed down a case of empty green Coca-Cola bottles and came straight towards his son-in-law. He thrust his face close to Jonas's. "What in the shit's the matter with you, boy? You get up with a fart crossways or something? Why ain't ya in church where ya belong?"

Pale-faced and silent, Jonas stared at Ephraim.

Ephraim wrinkled his nose. "Shee-ut. I can smell what's got in to you, boy."

Jonas looked away, drawing his hand across his forehead. Matteo watched as the others began to drift away towards the bridge below, all except the twins who went off slowly in the opposite direction. When they'd all gone, Ephraim struck again.. "What you got to say for yourself then?"

"I…I wasn't right this morning."

Ephraim's face twitched into a half smile. "Yeah. And I reckon you weren't too damn good last night, neither." His eyes flickered briefly in Matteo's direction, before turning back to Jonas. "How much of that old pudding grease you had this morning then?"

Jonas's torso gave a violent heave upwards and he clutched his mouth. He took six stumbling steps before falling to his hands and knees and vomiting copiously over a tangle of honeysuckle and blackberries.

Matteo turned away. All he could hear was Jonas gasping for air. He was walking away when Jonas called out. "Hey, Matthew!"

Matteo paused and glanced back over his shoulder.

Jonas was still on his knees. "Don't tell Esther about this, will ya? Ya promise? Ya won't tell her, will ya?"

Matteo shook his head and started back home.

As Matteo neared the crest that had yielded such a splendid view of his parents' old home, he hoped the stillness of the morning—washed to stunning clarity by the sunlight—would refresh his mind. To his disappointment, he saw the small grey silhouette of Marcus's back, perched on the boulder where his mother's rosary had been hidden.

Matteo considered re-tracing his steps down the hill towards the bridge and returning to his house by the main road. Or perhaps he could skirt the field quietly, skulking through the woods in a broad arc and avoiding the boy altogether…

But why avoid Marcus on account of his father's insulting behaviour? Matteo shook his head at his own foolishness. Instead of hiding, he would try out the local manner he'd just learnt. "Why aren't you in church?" he called.

Marcus looked around. "I done went" he said. "Kids is only supposed to go to Sunday school and all. Sermons and stuff is for grown-ups."

Matteo sat on one of the rocks. "Your father didn't go today?" he asked nonchalantly.

"Naw," Marcus said without looking up. "He pretty near always goes, except he was sick again last night."

Matteo recalled what Marcus had told him about his father's fits of sorrow, and much was suddenly made clear to him.

Marcus was holding the spinning top Matteo had given him. "You've brought your top with you," Matteo said. "It won't be much good up here."

Marcus just looked out over the sunlit fields.

"Have you decided what to put on the four sides?"

"Naw. Not yet." Marcus stood up, leaned towards Matteo and whispered, "I asked Daddy and that's what made him sick."

The boy's eyes were filling with tears. Matteo turned away, pretending not to notice. "What did you say to him?"

"I just said that you give me a square top with a hex sign on it, and that I was to find something to write on the sides. He said that I sure ought to give it back, 'cause if he ever got hold of it he'd up and throw it in the crick. Then he went out of the house and this morning Mama said he was sick again and we was all going to church without him."

Matteo glanced at the top, and saw that the spindle was now attached. A streaked dew-stain on its side told him that Marcus must have hidden the toy with his other treasures.

Marcus sat down again and pointed to the hex sign. "Besides, I been looking at this thing, and I done figured out that it ain't magic at all."

"No?"

The boy raised his eyes towards the panorama at their feet. "Naw. It's a map."

Matteo fell silent for a moment. The boy had believed in witchcraft; how much credit could be given to his imagination? There was only one way to find out. "A map of what?"

"Of all this." Marcus moved his arm in a broad sweep indicating the entire vista before them. "Look here."

Matteo slid down the boulder and looked over Marcus's shoulder. Marcus went on, raising and lowering his finger between the countryside and the spinning top, as if he were stitching the landscape to its image on the toy. "All these yellow bits is cornfields."

Matteo looked from the toy to the surrounding countryside and began to see what Marcus meant. Allowing for the passage of time, and granting that the painted yellow lines had a symmetry that the fields didn't quite possess, it was plain that the two corresponded in spirit.

"The green ones is where the other fields is, and the long blue lines and circles is where the cricks and ponds go."

Matteo followed one of these lines with his eyes, moving along the trail past the bridge where he had spoken to the men, and beyond to where it was joined by the second line of the stream above his own house. "Then the red squares and diamonds are houses?"

"Yeah, and barns and sheds and stuff. Some of them I reckon is gone—tore down a long time ago. Like this one." He pointed to a square. "That old place fell in before I was born and ain't nothing left now except stones and all."

"And what about the white background?" Matteo asked.

"Well, that's trees mostly. There use to be more than there is now."

Wondering how there could ever have been more trees than he saw now, Matteo gestured to Marcus to let him examine the top more closely. Holding it in his hands, he lifted his small silver glasses up on to his forehead in the same way that he had seen Nonno do as an old man.

There it was, the tiny pattern that he had painted himself, copying a design the details of which he had learned by rote, and yet one with a meaning that had remained obscure until its significance had been unlocked by a boy.

He turned it repeatedly in his hands: there was his house, there Jonas's, here and there his neighbours' farms and fields, little altered in the decades since his father's death.

Running his fingers over the glossy surface, he paused when his fingertip came to rest on a small black dot. Looking closer, he remembered that on these large copies of the hex sign he routinely put four such spots in the design, at what had before seemed like randomly chosen places, repeated — like the entire pattern — from memory. He looked again over the surrounding hills and valleys, seeking whatever those dots might represent.

There was nothing, and he turned back to Marcus. "What are the black spots?"

Marcus leaned in to see what Matteo meant. "Oh, them's the lar trees I told ya about."

Matteo handed the top back to the boy and stepped down from the rocks. Surely the mountains held countless clusters of laurel trees? How could anyone, even someone in the clutch of a primitive superstition, believe that some of them were lucky? Had his father believed in such things?

Matteo turned and beckoned to Marcus. "Follow me."

He set off along the edge of the field towards the fringes of the forest, striding quickly, with Marcus jogging to keep up. In a few minutes they were at the far end of the field, at the edge of a belt of trees that widened until it blended with the forested mountainside. Matteo pressed on, his feet swishing through dead leaves, and peered intently into the tangle of trees amongst which nothing but wild animals ever grazed.

Before long, the wooded slope began to curve around to his left, slipping away into a rounded depression that was roofed with orange pools of leaf-borne sunlight. Here, on the sheltered side, catching the sun for the longest part of the day, he found a small knot of laurel trees. He went in among them, stroking their bark and leaves. These, at least, were not strangers in kind, and not one of them was taller than him.

He paused close to one of the trees and turned to Marcus. "These are laurel trees, I'm certain of it. I've known them ... all my life. If others are special, why aren't these?" Matteo motioned for Marcus to pass the top back, then looked closely at it once more. Just as he had expected, the cluster of laurels where they stood was not marked by a black spot on the map. The nearest was further up the hillside, where the ground curved to the left, looking outwards over the valley.

Marcus grasped the tree, putting his hand just below Matteo's. He shook the tree slightly, his mouth flickering into a grin. "Naw," he said. "This ain't a lar tree. This is a *larl* tree."

Matteo stared at the boy, his face tensing slightly with frustration.

"If you want to see the *lar* trees, I'll show them to ya. If ya promise not to tell nobody I did."

Matteo handed the toy back to Marcus, and nodded. In a flash, Marcus took off in front of him, heading further up the hill beyond a crescent of larger trees.

Before long, Matteo found himself on a tall escarpment looking almost due west. After the steep climb, he was not surprised by the direction he now faced, or by the fact that the ground lay so high above the valley floor. What struck him ,though, was that once more he had gained an unlooked-for perspective on his home.

From here, he could see the house clinging to the wooded hillside, and beyond it the channel of the mountain, rough-hewn by long-departed glaciers. Farther still, the wave-like line of the entire range rested in the violet-tinted haze that gave them their name.

The sight made him shake his head in wonder. He looked

back to see Marcus, twenty feet away and near a clump of boulders.

"Here it is," Marcus shouted, pointing to an immense tulip poplar tree rooted in a deep cup of earth.

Matteo looked up at the tree, the topmost branches of which must have been sixty feet over his head. Several smaller stumps stood rotting in the vicinity. The tree was once plainly part of a larger group that had grown up in the lee of the mountain.

Matteo grimaced and went over to where Marcus was standing. "So. Why is this tree special?"

Instead of answering, Marcus pointed to a spot on the tree bark fifteen feet above them, and three feet above the tree's lowest limb. As Matteo's gaze fell on the place indicated, he felt his blood stand still. There before him—in characters twelve inches tall—he read the letters: 'LAR'.

Matteo stood motionless. Leaves out of time whirled in his memory, stirring again the sound of his father's voice as he spoke his wife's name: *Lar.* It was undoubtedly how he had said the word, and Matteo was deeply moved by this new discovery. "Show me the map," he whispered.

The two of them studied the image until Matteo said, "Now let's find the others."

They went on around the broad and curving swing of the hillside until they reached a narrow declivity separating them from the range of hills where they both lived. As they started towards the bottom of this channel, Matteo saw a crooked, pie-slice-shaped glimpse of the mountains far away to the south of Ephraim's store.

Marcus stopped and touched Matteo on the forearm. "There it is." He pointed.

Matteo turned to see a clump of poplars towering above a forest of hickory, ash and second-growth oak, but he was unable to spot the exact tree Marcus indicated.

They continued down the hillside, crossed a flat rocky stream, and started up the opposite slope. Mid-way along the ascent, just as Matteo was glancing at the hex-signed toy and reassuring himself that its markings were accurate, Marcus stopped him.

"It's way up there." The boy shielded his eyes from the sun, and Matteo did likewise. It was still too bright: he saw nothing. He went around the tree until the sun was no longer in his eyes, and then saw a roughly carved 'R', then, 'A' and 'L'.

The letters were even further above the ground than before—maybe twenty-five feet up—and were wrapped around crookedly above the tree's third set of branches. Matteo knew that this usually meant that the tree had grown up exposed to more light, and he turned his back towards it to look out in the direction that the letters faced.

Through the black net of branches that stretched over the sky, he saw that the close valley he had just crossed, through which the southern horizon was partially visible, was shallow enough that the farther up the hill he went, the less it obstructed the view. This gave him an idea, and he gestured to Marcus to follow him.

Matteo went further along the hillside until he reached the crest. As he had expected, from here the entire panorama unfolded again and he could see the store at the junction where the valleys met, and fields in the distance that could have belonged to the twins Ira and Asa. The low rise masked Jonas's farm, and—to his satisfaction—his own house against the hillside opposite. He turned on his heel and—sure enough—the same perspective could be shared by anyone who looked from the place where his mother's initials were carved.

The location of the third of the LAR trees proved, now, to be no surprise. Matteo and Marcus had hiked through the forest, crossing the stream that had fed both moonshiners' stills and whose waters had helped Matteo to wash his home clean of its long neglect. They had reached a point on the ridge that lay half-way along the mountainside west of Matteo's house. The poplar trees here were fewer in number, and the tangle of undergrowth correspondingly thicker.

The third tree was by far the largest. Tall, straight and un-broken by limbs for more than twenty feet, the letters were carved only about two feet above his head. Once again, they were in the direction that faced his house, only the rooftop of which could be glimpsed below.

Stretching out his arm, Matteo traced the letters with his fingertip. More than twenty years of rain, wind and growth had done little to change their shape or obscure their mean-ing. They represented not just his mother's initials, but the sound of his father's voice, speaking the name of the woman he loved.

On the day Matteo's mother left her home in Italy, both her own mother and her father had imagined that she would nev-er return in their lifetimes. Yet the grief they felt at losing their daughter, and the sorrow they knew when they imagined the grandchildren who might never know their true homeland, was softened by the joy in the young lovers' eyes. A few years later, when she returned to them a widow with an only son, their hearts were sunken in a grief that stained all their future happiness.

However much they tried to live the life of a family strength-ened by its younger generation, they were never without the long shadow of emptiness that clings to those who have lost someone they loved. Later, when his mother sickened and died, a hollow peace—easily mistaken for resignation—fell over their existence.

They took some comfort in the knowledge that those who had loved most, might now find rest in one another's spirit. But they also discovered the peculiar sadness of old people thrust into the role of parents: that no matter how much they might love, they can neither give, nor be, all that a parent could.

Matteo turned to find Marcus. The boy was sitting on a rotting stump, looking east into the fields and woods beyond Matteo's house. As Matteo watched, the boy's mouth opened into a wide yawn. He had walked far—even for a boy born and bred to those wild hills—and he could not have eaten for most of the day.

Matteo chided himself. Hadn't Esther blamed him for not paying more attention to the needs of the children who trusted him? He went down the hill and knelt beside his young friend. "Are you hungry?"

The boy took longer than strictly necessary to reply, particularly when the answer was so plain. Matteo amused himself by imagining the options running through Marcus's head: would he have to go home? Or, was he being offered lunch? Did this mean a final end to the walk?

"Yeah," he said at last.

The two of them crossed the fields and wove through the stands of trees separating them from Matteo's house, neither one having much to say.

When they got back, Marcus headed straight for the kitchen door, where he waited. Matteo—in the midst of reverie—had forgotten his suggestion of food. He stood at the corner of the porch near the swing, from where he studied the view opposite the house. Eventually, Marcus followed him outside.

"Anyway," Matteo said, "you can always show me the other tree later."

"What other tree?"

Matteo turned and looked at him. "The other LAR tree."

"There ain't no more."

"There must be." Frowning, Matteo took the top once more.

"Look." He pointed. "There is a fourth black spot. There has always been one there in the pattern."

Marcus peered at the map and then shook his head. "Well, there sure ain't no more LAR trees that I know of."

"Have you ever looked?"

Marcus said nothing.

Matteo turned the top around in his hands to try and read it more clearly. How charming it was, he thought, that his own house should be the centre of the map, and that the four directions represented by the trees should only be readable by someone like his father, who knew the terrain well.

"There," he said, "the fourth tree ought to be over there somewhere."

Marcus looked from the toy to the long slope opposite Matteo's house. "Well, there sure is a lot a little poplars and all, but there ain't no big ones."

Matteo gazed across the distance. There were no large trees, but hundreds of small ones had pushed their way up through a clutter of underbrush. As he scanned the area, he caught a flash of movement: someone was coming up the hill from the lower ground to the left. The figure disappeared and then reappeared, and Matteo recognised Esther, most likely in search of her errant son.

Seeing her climbing the hillside, her hair aglow in the late afternoon sun, he was reminded of the last time he had seen her there. It was the day they had spoken about love and about loneliness, not in the shade of a powerful tree, but near the margins of a tangle of small unkempt saplings whose name he didn't know.

Then he remembered, and shivered slightly.

They were a copse of pawpaw trees.

Chapter Eleven

"Matteo," the voice called. "Matteo."

A delicate, trembling happiness unlike anything he had ever known thrilled throughout Matteo's body, all the way to his fingertips, where it rested. He stretched out his arm across the bed to where she had lain, to where the crease in the sheets had captured the impression of her body. The room was as white as flour and the few pieces of chestnut furniture, all stained as dark as the earth, stood out proudly.

"Matteo," she called again.

Naked, he stood up and went to the chair, cutting across shafts of sunlight that cascaded from the half-open window to the floor. He pulled on his clothes and glanced outside. He could just hear the murmur of her voice speaking to someone he couldn't see.

The freshness of the midsummer morning swept into his

lungs, bringing with it the fragrance of basil from the court-
yard below and orange blossom from the orchards beyond.
For a moment he thought he glimpsed her everywhere—in
everything—and the memory of the warmth of his lover stole
over him again.

"Matteo." The voice was nearer now.

She was a year younger than he, and they had been introduced by the sister of a friend. Her eyes were concentric
circles of green and brown and green; she had not mistaken,
nor misunderstood, the earnestness with which he sought to
determine their true colour. And now he had woken in her
house.

She had brought him here on purpose, so that he might see
her amidst the world that had shaped her feelings. It had been
her family's home for generations. Paintings of her ancestors
hung on the walls, as did coats-of-arms. There was even a tiny
almost-black room consecrated as a chapel.

Nonno's good fortune in the post-war boom meant that Matteo's own family was at least as wealthy as hers. He also knew
that her unconventional family had alienated themselves, to
some extent, from others of their class. Yet to him, their qual-
ity showed in their manner as much as in their breeding, in
their persons as much as their possessions. So now he had
come to be her second lover, and she his first.

"Matteo." Her voice was just below the window.

Barefoot, he trod lightly down the back stairs and on to the
cold flagstones of the kitchen. The untempered light hung
in columns through the hallway as he moved towards the
house's wide doors and on towards the terrace where he expected to find her. The gentlest of breezes still lingered in the
dark folds of the door curtains when he stepped outside.

The woman turned to him and smiled. It was Esther.

Matteo sat up in the darkness of his room. He passed his hand over his face to dismiss the last traces of a dream he had dreamt often in the past three years, and that had now become transfigured by the present. He glanced at his watch on the bedside table. It was three a.m. His sense of time and place returned, and so did the previous day's brooding that had lain guttering in his mind while he fell asleep.

Unable to rest and unwilling to think, Matteo dressed and went downstairs to the kitchen. The black landscape beyond the window reminded him of the night sea. He turned on the light, wondering how far his window could be seen into the night.

He opened the cupboard door to take out a fresh tin of coffee. Only two tins were left. Apprehension, another grain of sand, slipped into the mechanism of his mind.

With the last swallow of coffee still warm on his lips, Matteo shouldered his axe and went outside. A gauze of cloud hung in strands over the east, but elsewhere the sky was clear.

Not knowing where else to roam, he turned upstream and stepped from rock to rock, heading for the two clusters of apple trees. As he neared the first of the enclosures, he paused.

The starlight seemed to have drawn itself together into the paleness of the apple blossoms, shining against the darkness. He wondered whether these trees had been as beautiful to the moonshiners, or if the men had only seen them as beacons in the night.

With the dark-chilled wind blowing through his hair, Matteo knelt down, picked up a stone and threw it into the stream thirty feet in front of him. It landed with a small *plish*. A larger answering splash sounded from a few feet farther on, followed by silence. He decided he must have knocked something into the water. A branch, perhaps. He went on.

Moments later, he heard another splash, as of something

pulling itself out of the water and on to the bank. Peace returned. Matteo took his axe into both hands and crept closer.

Leaves rustled on the left side of the stream, and he saw an animal like a black stone scuttle along in the underbrush. It went on for a few feet and then hesitated.

Whatever it was turned and made a noise halfway between a growl and a cry of pain. Matteo looked into the glint of its yellow-green eyes before it swung about, limping sideways, travelled another few feet, fell down and got up again. In a moment, it vanished into the darkness.

Aimless and frustrated, he crossed to the right bank of the stream and started up the hillside. Being in no hurry and not knowing the way, he soon found himself in a high place he didn't recognise.

From this vantage point, he could see three clusters of blue lights glowing at different spots on the slope of the valley below, and he guessed these must be farmers already up to milk their cows. Soon, Jonas would be awake too, and preparing to face another day of work. What should Matteo say to him when he saw him next? Would the whole experience pass into silence?

Tiers of cloud, fading to cream, lay over the horizon, and Matteo saw a clearing in the trees farther down the slope where, if he couldn't see the sun come up, he could at least watch it pour over the forest above him.

Crossing a barbed wire fence, Matteo found himself in a field close to the pile of stones where he had once sat with Esther. Uneasiness churned his stomach. He had not wanted to return to this place, especially since he had discovered that the cursed pawpaw copse held some peculiar significance.

"Foolish!" he said aloud, surprised to hear himself speaking English alone. This was the best viewpoint he would find around here, and he might as well go.

Walking faster than before, he headed straight to the highest point of the field, and climbed to the summit of the rocks.

Fully exposed to the wind now, Matteo shivered slightly as the cold air swept round him. Perhaps he had been stupid, coming here. Esther had said that Jonas used to visit this spot, and Marcus had told him that his father still did so, to be alone with his sadness.

Matteo was not the man to intrude on Jonas to satisfy his own curiosity, least of all now when he knew his friend to be at low ebb. He glanced around, reassuring himself again that he was alone, then set about choosing a comfortable-looking rock from which to watch over his own and his neighbour's homes.

As he moved, Matteo felt something shifting like tiny ball bearings beneath his boots. He pressed his palm against the ground, and—wet with dew—several stuck to his fingers. Holding his hand up to the growing light, Matteo saw that the tiny beads were pawpaw seeds. He shuffled his feet and a multitude of them scattered into the tall grass below him.

Yet above him was nothing but the sky. The fruit had not fallen here; something or someone had brought it. He looked around to where the paw-paw trees grew, to the place where Esther had supposed him to be a prowling animal.

Letting the seeds sift through his fingers, Matteo recalled the original contents of his toy bag. Maybe the pawpaw trees had been important to his father after all.

He glanced around to make sure he was still alone, and then descended from the rocks and went once again to the grove of trees.

The dim light, his recent brush with the sick animal, and the memory of his first visit to this spot—all combined to make his senses acute. Once again he heard the crackle of twigs and branches under his feet, more of them than he'd expected, even under fruit trees like this.

He bent down to examine some of the larger sticks. All were rotted by countless seasons of exposure. A few of the largest still had remnants of bark clinging to them and he examined these carefully, holding them up to the light.

To Matteo's surprise, most of the pieces were not from the pawpaw trees, but from something else entirely. And many of the branches at his feet, now choked by tufted weedy grass, were simply too large to have come from the trees that now surrounded him. What could it mean? Matteo clenched his teeth in frustration, and looked around him. Could this have been the site of a much larger tree, some time in the past?

But of course, why shouldn't it have done so? A tree might be a monument, he told himself, but it was hardly a permanent one. Perhaps a LAR tree had stood here once and long since fallen, or been cut down by people unconcerned with its meaning. The idea pleased him.

The wind was shifting, and he heard the soft *pang-pang* of cow-bells from the herds below. The first clear signs of dawn showed in the sky above him, lighting branches and buds that were opening into tiny leaves. He had seen the seasons nearly through.

Matteo crunched about on the dead sticks, occasionally turning back to the forest behind him, slowly losing interest in whether any of the trees there had bark that matched the branch in his hand.

A gust of cool, aromatic scent contrasted with the gradually warming air, and Matteo sniffed to find the direction from which the fragrance was coming—and saw a cluster of shadows clinging to the fringe of the woods. He had forgotten that this was a place where cedars grew, though he had noticed the evergreens when he was last here in the autumn, and thought then how strange and remote they seemed.

He stood close to them now, and brushed his hand against

the thick net of their foliage. Drops of dew clinging to them shivered and fell to the ground.

Matteo had noticed before that, despite the toil it cost the farmers to claim their land from the wilderness, they all treated the margins between the fields as dumping grounds. Everywhere he had seen the detritus of their work: stones, stumps, coils of rusted wire, rotting wood and other waste, littering the boundaries. So he was not surprised that the stand of cedars had been allowed to spring up, screening the pile of waste behind them.

Hidden behind the trees was a jumble of smashed metal sheeting, discarded buckets, and some twisted coils of pipe made green, it seemed, by the half-light of the morning.

Curious, Matteo stepped closer and rubbed some of the pipe, transferring verdigris to his fingers. The whole tangle seemed to be the oxidising remains of some failed plumbing experiment.

Stepping sideways, he winced as something smacked into his leg below the knee. He rubbed the place with one hand and played the other about on the grass until he found the rim of an old barrel hoop, which had swung up when he stepped on it.

As he brushing the rust off his hands, it occurred to him that he had seen hoops like this in one other place.

In an instant, he understood.

Ephraim had said that among his neighbours, copper was valuable enough for people to harvest—or steal—for sale as scrap. He had also said that he had helped Jonas dismantle the still that had belonged to Jonas's father. Most likely, Jonas—through fear of detection—had never sold this metal, but secreted it here where it might be forgotten.

Satisfied with this deduction, Matteo kicked at one of the bucket-contraptions and watched it roll down the pile of rubbish until it snagged on a length of rope. Seized by a sudden

desire to see what was inside the copper cauldron, Matteo
tried to pull it closer by tugging at one end of the rope. Although he tugged hard, the rope refused to give way, so he
looked for an end that he could untangle.

Kicking around in the rubble and weeds, he found one at
last, but it was looped through a steel ring driven into the
ground by a stake. Jonas must have done this job with his
usual thoroughness, Matteo decided, and secured the clutter
to keep it from blowing around. Abandoning the project of
the rope, he decided to climb on to the pile and pick up the
piece of copper by hand.

He sunk the toe of his boot into a chink between two pieces of stacked wood and tried to raise himself. As he did so,
the entire stack—soaking and mushy with rot—sagged and
threatened to roll towards him, and he stepped back smartly.
One end of the old cord-pile was propped up on a chunk of
tree trunk, too big and too gnarled for splitting. Thinking he
would use this as a step, Matteo pushed away the remaining
lengths of wood, exposing the slippery wet bark of a huge log
at the base of the pile. As soon as he saw it, he forgot everything else, because the conviction gripped him that this could
be the missing LAR tree.

Working in the growing, honey-coloured light, Matteo
pushed away bundles of broken limbs, briars and weeds,
slowly uncovering the enormous trunk, but constantly chal-
lenged and frustrated by the lengths of rope that zigzagged
over the mass, making it impossible to clear completely.

Careless of the consequences, Matteo hefted his axe and
chopped through the nearest span of rope. He raised the axe
for a second blow, but something caught his eye: new-born
sunlight, flaring in a white line across the axe-head.

He must have struck something hard enough to put a long
scratch on the steel. But surely he had aimed his blow safely
into the massive trunk? He knelt down to see what he could

have hit, and found that the log was scored by a straight black groove more than a quarter of an inch wide. On one side, this cut ran about two thirds of the way through the wood. From the other, a wide jagged piece of iron protruded: the broken blade of an old-fashioned cross-cut saw.

Matteo looked at the disc-shaped slab he had used as a step. Several similar pieces lay about, wooden nickels scattered from a giant's hand. A few showed the angled bites where someone had split off portions for firewood, before abandoning the rest.

Matteo sat down. He was getting tired and frustrated, now. The only sounds were the songs of birds in the forest above him, and the occasional lowing of a cow from one of the fields below. He was hungry, his hands and clothes were smeared with grime and—worst of all—he was growing increasingly uncomfortable about the fact that he was trespassing.

This was the second time that his curiosity had led to embarrassment, and in almost this exact spot. The act of yielding to that curiosity felt like a betrayal of something in himself that he had once greatly esteemed. And yet his knowledge of deceptions, and of self-deceptions in particular, motivated him to search, even though the searching might be painful.

Light sparkled on the treetops, and Matteo stood up to get a better view. He stepped forward, towards the end of the log beyond the point where it had been cut by the saw. The timber gave way with a dull cracking noise and he fell heavily on to his hands and knees amidst the clutter.

Angry at his own negligence, he checked the end of the tree that had snapped off under him. Two thirds of the wood inside was smoky-brown with rot, down to the point where the broken blade lay embedded across it in a rusty stripe. The splintered piece he had stood on, eighteen inches thick and nearly two feet long, lay on its round side. He could see now that the log had once been raised at this end on to another smaller piece, so that chunks could be sawn off completely on to the ground. This alone had probably kept the broken piece from turning into a softening crumble like the rest of the log.

His anger passed, turning to amusement at his own folly, and Matteo—still sitting on the ground—put his foot on the heavy chunk and rolled it towards some weeds. With each revolution, the letters 'LAR' flashed into sight and then disappeared.

He jumped up, hurried to where the chunk of wood had come to rest, and turned it back towards him. It was the fourth of the trees he sought, and there was his mother's name. But he shrank back as he touched the word, for just below it, carved in the same hand, he also read the name, 'ISAAC'.

For a long while, Matteo could do nothing. He found himself unable to move, staring at the two words carved into the bark. Confusion, doubt, suspicion and rage washed over him. He imagined every possible play of circumstances that could have led to this second name appearing on the tree, but nothing could smother the realisation that it had not been his father who had wrought these strange love-tokens. In Matteo's mind, George Durante became what he had never been before: the dupe of the people who still shared his secrets.

For the first time, Matteo realised how badly he needed to know how his father had died. He looked around him at the silent, pitiless forest, at the fields that had been his home. He knew from his own experience how reluctant the world was to yield up the things it held. So it was with the people he lived among: reticent, superstitious, purposefully forgetful, afraid. Whatever they knew, they would scarcely share it with him.

He wanted to turn to this emptiness and cry out, but instead, his eyes fell on the axe that lay propped against the rotting hulk of timber. It had been this that had excited so much talk about him when he first arrived, giving his neighbours the impression that he was neither helpless, nor lazy nor a fool. He took up the axe by the handle and rapped it twice against the trunk, which answered with a hollow clunk. As the wood vibrated, there fell at his feet the jagged piece of metal that had drawn the long scratch on the axe's head.

Matteo bent down and picked up the broken rusty blade. It was from a cross-cut saw — a type of cutter practically extinct now, because it took the strength and rhythm of two people — one pulling at either end.

Matteo paused as the image of two men cutting down the tree flashed into his mind. This possibility, more than any need to know who Isaac was, made him gather as much of the scattered debris as he could, and to turn his back on the daylight that had grown up around him.

He could think of only one person in the vicinity who might be able to tell him who had helped to destroy the largest of the LAR trees. Ephraim had helped Jonas dismantle his father's still, and Ephraim had told Matteo outright that the poisoned-stream story was untrue. If this was Jonas's field, and if he had held one end of the saw, then it must have been Ephraim who held the other.

As Matteo went down the steep decline, he turned his face away from the blue house towards the direction of the cross-roads that lay just out of sight behind the next hill.

The laughter of the birds troubled him with the same faint note of his mother's voice, and the long shadow of a cloud brushed the fields growing green with new hay.

Chapter Twelve

Ephraim's shop was closed.

Frustrated with knocking, Matteo pounded the heel of his hand against the door. A tiny trickle of sweat eased slowly down his back; the day was growing warmer. He could hear the purring of a dove 'calling in the rain.'

He glanced at the little group of trees near the spot where, the previous Sunday, he had spoken to the other men. A bright triangle now shone through their shade. Matteo went towards the light.

Behind the place where he himself had stood before, he saw a towering cluster of green briar canes that sprang up from behind a white board fence. At the end of the fence was a small wooden gate that swung from a massive creosote-painted post. Lying on top was a wide plank, where a black and grey-striped cat sat washing itself sleepily.

As Matteo neared the gate, the cat paused and looked at him.

It stood up, arching its back in a slow stretch, and appeared friendly enough, but as Matteo reached to pet the creature, it jumped down heavily and disappeared behind the briars.

Matteo opened the gate. Beyond was a sloping square of lawn edged with flowers, behind which ran another angle of the white board fence that separated the dooryard from the vegetable patch. The neatness of it all surprised Matteo—the garden was a complete contrast to the tangled woodland just beyond its boundaries.

He followed the path around the house and on to the shaded back porch. The back door was open, except for the outer screen door which was crudely painted with a scene that included a carriage and a covered bridge.

The porch was furnished with two wicker chairs and a table. On the table were a box of matches, a leather pouch, and a home-made pipe that caught Matteo's eye.

He stepped up to the porch, went to the table and picked up the pipe. It was heavier than it looked, and its bowl, blackened by fire and handling, faded into a cherry stem that was also black with long use at the end. But what struck him was the circular embellishment on the bottom of the bowl. The decoration was grey and soiled like the rest of the pipe, but it was plainly a hex sign. It was partially worn away, but enough remained to tell Matteo that the design was nothing like the ones he had painted himself.

From the corner of one eye, he caught movement. He turned to see that someone had come into the garden from another direction and was now leaning through the board fence near the woods, apparently picking flowers from a tall, yellow-green bush.

Matteo put the pipe down and went to the edge of the porch. He cleared his throat. "Excuse me."

There was no response. Matteo coughed and called a little louder, "Excuse me."

The person, whom he judged to be a girl of about Ruth Ann's age and stature, still showed no signs of acknowledging his presence.

Annoyed, Matteo jumped down from the porch and strode towards her. Compared to the few other girls of this age he had seen, this one seemed peculiarly dressed. She was smaller and slighter than he had first thought, and wore an ankle-length calico dress with long sleeves, and what he deemed was a ridiculously large bonnet.

"Have you seen Ephraim?" he demanded loudly.

The girl turned around, and Matteo was shocked to behold one of the oldest faces he had ever seen. Cramped and toothless, her mouth puckered round in a narrow purplish hole, and the web of lines that marked out her eyes was so tightened by squinting that she seemed to have no eyes at all. She rested a blue arching hand on the board fence and faced Matteo calmly.

"How do," she said with a voice through which the wind whistled.

Matteo stammered, "I'm looking for Ephraim."

She raised her fist to her ear, frowned and tilted her head towards him. He repeated himself loudly until she closed the grey specks of her eyes and nodded twice. She then put out her hand to Matteo and beckoned for him to take from her whatever it was she held. Opening up her fingers in his palm, she dropped there a tuft of small yellow-green leaves.

She said nothing, but walked stiffly towards the house, stopping once and turning to beckon Matteo to follow.

As she neared the white glare of the window frame, she stopped as the striped cat re-appeared to rub up and down her legs. She turned again and looked at Matteo.

Unsure what to do, Matteo went closer, and she tapped her fist up and down on a silvered shelf of wood that had been fixed to a frame just below the window, where the sunshine was most intense.

On the shelf were arranged several rows of leaves like the ones Matteo held in his hand, all neatly laid out to dry in the sun. As the driest ones were near the top, Matteo spread out his handful along the bottom. By the time he had finished, the old woman had left him, and disappeared on to the porch where she sat in one of the chairs, filling her pipe.

With increasing frustration, Matteo mounted the steps to where she sat and watched as her crooked fingers deftly played a match into flame.

"Do you know where Ephraim is?" he asked.

A puff of grey smoke slipped out from between her lips and the pipe stem. "Yep."

"Then why won't you tell me?"

"Well, who says I weren't going to tell yeh?"

"Why have you waited so long then?"

She looked at him a moment and took the pipe from her mouth. "'Cause you wouldn't know if I told yeh ten times."

"What?"

"You know where my boy Sotz keeps his hogs?"

Matteo looked at her with bewilderment and shook his head. She put the pipe back in her mouth and muttered, "No, I didn't expect yeh did, and that's why I knowed I'd better sit down to tell yeh."

Standing above her, Matteo could smell the dark, bitter smoke from her pipe. She crumpled up into a powder some of the leaves she had taken from the plank where they dried and poured them into the pouch. The cat lolled on the bottom shelf of the table, proudly exposing an abdomen distended by the litter of kittens it carried.

"Will he be back soon?" Matteo asked.

"Who? Sotz?"

"Ephraim. I want to see Ephraim."

She grinned. "That is Sotz. That's what we called him since he was little. Sotz is yeast, and he's just like yeast." She leaned forward. "Yeh-goin' to sit down, so a body can tell yeh, or what?"

With puzzling pieces of the old woman's directions in his mind, Matteo headed off back over the bridge towards his own house, but instead of following his former road, he turned left, on the uphill fork that circled behind Jonas's farm.

He soon came to the opening in the roadside fence that the old woman had described. The entrance to the field was barred by a series of slotted posts, linked by poles fitted into the grooves. Each of the poles was more than twelve feet long; some were crumbling with rot while others were sappy and green. It was a gate unlike any Matteo had ever seen.

Matteo climbed onto the lowest pole and scanned the field beyond. The land was already disappearing under the green shoots of new-sown grain; further off, it vanished altogether in the cover of the woods. He could see no signs of habitation, not even the kind of rude structure that might have sheltered livestock. Perhaps he had become lost, he thought. Or perhaps he had misunderstood, or simply been misled.

The only way to find out was to continue a little further, up the incline of the field to where he might be able to see further.

As his feet touched the ground, a scream tore the silence of the woods ahead of him. Matteo froze. Whatever made that sound was crying out in terror. It was not human, though. He strode across the field, hurrying towards the sound. Another fence stood between the crop and the woodland, and beyond that was a stone enclosure. Something orange flashed above the stones, and then vanished.

Matteo stooped to pass between the taut barbed strands of the fence. A second wild scream came from within the stone paddock, followed by the unmistakable squealing and grunting of pigs. The orange cap appeared above the wall again, and under it was Ephraim's face.

Matteo continued up the hill, moving around the pigyard in search of the entrance. The wooden gate was just around the corner, and outside the gate clustered a small herd of pigs, just where he had *not* expected to find them.

The larger pigs startled at his approach, and ran squealing into the trees. Two of the younger, smaller pigs seemed unable to keep up with the others, and ran along stiffly with their hindquarters swathed in blood.

Matteo went to the gate, and was just in time to see Esther tighten her grip on another pig's forelegs as Ephraim pushed a key-shaped knife into the animal's scrotum. There was a spurt of blood as Ephraim drew back the knife, together with two bluish testicles. The pig kept squirming as Ephraim made a few more nicking cuts, dropped the excised organs into a bucket and then, laying aside the knife, used a rag to splash a brownish fluid over the pig's open wound.

Esther and Ephraim released the animal, and the awful scream was repeated for the third time as it sped towards the gate where Matteo stood. He stepped aside as Ephraim pushed the gate open, his orange cap bobbing above the wall again.

Ephraim set a blood-soaked hand on the stones and studied Matteo. "Well, sir, what in the shit's done brung you up here?"

"I want something," Matteo answered.

Ephraim grinned. "The store's closed this morning, till all this fixing's done."

"I don't want to buy anything."

Ephraim turned to Esther and laughed. "Hee-heeuh. Shit,

boy, only thing that's free's advice. That, and mountain oys-ters." He pointed to the bucket. "You can have a couple of them for free, if ya want 'em."

"Daddy!" Esther chided.

Matteo looked at her just as she brushed away a lock of hair that had stuck to her face. Her palm and fingers were coated with filth. Quickly, he turned his attention to the distant range of hills.

Ephraim jerked his head towards the sheer drop of moun-tainside, where a vast, smooth blue-green stone formed the fourth side of the pig's pen.

"This is called Hog Rock. Some of our people built these walls a long time ago. One of them was so proud that he put his initials in it up there." He pointed. "There's another one up the mountain called Wolf Rock, and another one further down called Crow Rock, but I don't expect they ever did none of this work at either one."

"I want to know about a tree," Matteo said.

Esther came a little closer.

Ephraim rolled his eyes to look at the woods surrounding them. "Well then, we'll have plenty to talk about."

Matteo bolted the gate so that he could lean on it, uncon-sciously shutting Esther and Ephraim inside.

"There was a tree," he said, "that used to grow at the top of the hillside above Jonas's farm. A huge tree — a pop-lar — which was cut down a long time ago. It was cut down with a saw; a kind of saw that takes two people to work — one to pull at either end." Matteo paused, waiting for Ephraim to speak.

Ephraim just stared at Matteo with the strange wide-eyed way he had, and said nothing.

Matteo asked him point-blank. "Did you help to cut it down?"

Ephraim's double-chin sagged towards his collar as he gave an open-mouthed smile.

"Boy, I ain't used no cross-cut saw since Pa died, and I sure as Hell didn't use none up there in them woods of his."

"But you did help break up his father's still?"

"Hell, yes, I did."

"Well, parts of the still were piled on top of that tree."

"Well, sir—Matthew—I just flung it up on the pile of junk where the boy told me too, I didn't look inside the junk." He turned to his daughter. "Hell, Esther, you got Dick Tracy for a neighbour."

Esther smiled wanly, and looked at Matteo. "What you want to know?" she said.

"Who helped Jonas cut down that tree?"

She met Matteo's eyes for a moment, then looked away. "'Deed," she whispered. "I don't even know what you're a-talking about."

Matteo nodded his head cynically. "So."

The pigs had now returned and were snuffling for acorns among the leaves behind him. Matteo glanced at them and muttered, "Who was Isaac?"

"What'd you say?" Ephraim asked.

Matteo looked at him and then at Esther, saying nothing.

Esther answered. "He was…" Her voice caught and she cleared her throat. "Jonas's daddy. He was Jonas's daddy."

For the rest of that day, Matteo did nothing but walk and rest under the trees. From Hog Rock he followed the collapsing line of locust posts that marked the edges of his own over-grown fields, making his way eventually back to his house, where he stopped long enough to pack his mother's rosary, a loaf of bread, some of Ephraim's Lebanon bologna, and two bottles of wine.

Before long, he stood once again at the viewpoint from where Marcus had first deciphered the meaning of the hex-signs. He stood for a while looking out over the wide encir-cling hills, resting his eyes on the different landmarks spread before him. The season was advancing with surprising speed; he had first seen this spot only a matter of days before, but the sun already seemed to be swinging further around the sky in the journey from spring to summer.

Matteo lifted the stones where the boy had hidden the spin-ning top, and rifled Marcus's trove. The top was no longer there. This hardly mattered, though. Matteo was now so fa-miliar with the toy that he could picture its design clearly in his mind.

Marcus had oriented him within the scope of that map by comparing its design with the pattern of the world below. But a map, he thought, ought to have reference points of its own. One by one he pictured the placement of the LAR trees.

When he had imagined all of them, it was clear that they coincided roughly with the points of a compass. Could the whole thing have been some kind of moonshiner code?

The original image had been first painted by his father, as far as Matteo could tell. If this were true, then his father *must* have known about the LAR trees—including the one with his neighbour's name carved just below his wife's.

By the time he had reached the nearest of the trees—the first one that Marcus had shown him—Matteo had drunk half a bottle of wine. There was no mistaking the fact that the letters were shaped by the same hand that had carved the oth-ers, including the one above Jonas's field.

Matteo's eyes played back and forth between his mother's carved name, and the house she had lived. It was strange, he thought, that if the tree was meant to be a guidepost for others, that the letters should be on the side nearest the house, and not facing outwards, where they could have been seen more easily by someone walking towards them. Matteo tried to picture the other two trees, to recall how the carving had been oriented, but he couldn't remember. He drained the remainder of the first bottle, and headed further up the mountain.

Standing once again on the hillside that gave him the best view of the second LAR tree, Matteo was re-assured to see that as before, his mother's name faced in the direction of the house. But how, he wondered, could a word that possessed no meaning except to a few people, carved so high above the forest floor, ever have held a practical use for anybody?

Speculating about its use as a symbol, Matteo put his hand into his bag and fumbled at the beads of his mother's rosary. He drew out the second bottle of wine and held it in a shaft of sunlight for a while, admiring the ruby glow it brought to his hand. Although he wasn't thirsty, the sheer beauty of the wine in the bottle made him draw the cork and have another long drink.

A short while later, Matteo was sitting beneath the third of the LAR trees, facing his house, his mother's name in the bark not far above his head. The second wine bottle lay at his feet, empty, and its suavity had combined with fatigue to drape a heavy curtain over his mind.

Ideas played about inside him like ghosts, sometimes taking on the colour of the moonlight he had seen, or the crimson of Ephraim's bloodstained hands. Abruptly, Matteo stood up, then went shakily onwards to where the fourth LAR tree lay in ruins.

It was evening by the time Matteo reached the forest edge where the cluster of pawpaw trees grew. The extra exertion of crossing Jonas's fence proved too much, and Matteo squatted down to vomit up the orts and lees of overindulgence.

Sick, quivering, and angry, he kicked at the stones around

the wide brown circle that marked where the tree had once been rooted. Looking out over the surrounding mountains, he felt himself to be like his family's blue house, at the centre point of something unnameable, unknowable. In a flash, he saw that the LAR trees were not the love-tokens he had taken them to be, but four posts in an invisible wall, drawn around his mother, holding her within. He thought he saw what had been intended for no one else's eyes—a pattern into which she had been locked by someone.

Not knowing what else to do, Matteo sat down and wept.

When he awoke, the sky over his head was dark. Venus hung her lamp in the west; several other stars came and went; and a desultory moon peeked in and out of the clouds. As he lifted his head, the weight of dying alcohol pushed down inside his brain, making him feel hot and cold at the same time. He pushed himself up with his hands and saw above him—seated on the rocks—the silhouette of a man, featureless against the darkness.

"Jonas?"

"I thought you was dead a-laying there till I heard ya a-snoring." Jonas's voice was kind.

"It was your father Isaac who carved the names on the LAR trees, wasn't it?"

There was a pause before Jonas whispered, "Yep."

"Why did he do it?"

"Aw, 'Why'd he do it, Why'd he do it…' I don't know. 'Cause he had to do something with his self. He just had to do something about it."

"About what?" Matteo asked.

Jonas spoke very slowly. "He was sick with that woman from the day she come here. I knowed it, Ma knowed it. But nobody else knew it. Least…" He paused and looked at Matteo. "He knew she didn't want him or nothing, 'cause she wanted your daddy so much. He worried his self half to death with a-thinking about her, a-walking 'round in the woods and not fit for a damn thing. Shit, I wasn't much more than a kid and I done most of the work for him. After a while he got to liking that old still again. Not cause he was much of a moonshiner or nothing, just 'cause…"

He stopped again, and his tone changed. "I reckon that he figured that them trees was, I don't know … something. That if your mammy went out of the house, they'd keep her close somehow, like they was a-looking down on her even though she couldn't see them or nothing."

He coughed, and Matteo waited for him to continue. Moonlight shone in the corners of Jonas's eyes as he re-traced the memory.

"Well, one night Daddy and me was out a-'coon hunting. We got up there to where the still was—his own still—and we heard something moving like, ya know. I was sure it was a 'coon, especially when I heard it come from up high in the trees." Jonas looked at Matteo. "Hunting 'coons means ya run them up in to the trees, mostly, then shoot them."

He looked away again into the darkness. "Anyway, I was just about to shoot when daddy up and grabs my gun and tells me to get on home, 'cause he didn't need me to do no more hunting. That was when he got interested in that old still again."

Jonas and Matteo stared at one another for a moment, and neither spoke. Jonas looked away first. "Well, moonshining ain't no easy thing to do, especially if ya don't want to get caught. But Daddy didn't have nobody to help him, see, so I used to go out on the nights he was a-working, and sit in the bushes up on the sides of the hills, just to make sure and all. He didn't know nothing about it, or I guess he'd have skint me alive for a-risking getting myself shot, but I just felt like I ought to. Well, most nights there weren't much to see, but then one night…" Jonas trailed off. Matteo sat up a little straighter. "One night, I heard something up there in the trees again. This time I didn't give a shit whether it was no 'coon or nothing, I thought it was somebody a-looking for Daddy down there. So I went on up the hill back there."

Jonas pointed, as rapt as if the scene were still before him. "Back behind where them apple trees stop I waited, and listened. Just like the last time, the noise was a-coming from up in the trees. I'd done got myself round so as the moon was a-shining behind me, and I could see somebody a-sitting up in the tree. I was a-shaking like I had a buck-fever, a-thinking I ought to shoot them or something, when I just sees Daddy a-getting closer too. I was nearly shittin' myself trying to get closer so as I could do something, when I heard Daddy say something."

"What did he say?" Matteo asked.

Jonas's voice was a whisper. "Lar."

"She was up in the tree? She was my father's lookout?"

Jonas nodded. For a long time he said nothing else, and Matteo could feel the tension growing between them.

"What else did he say?" he asked finally.

Jonas shook his head. "I ain't a-saying. No, sir, I ain't a-repeating it. It was just pitiful. He told her he'd do I don't know what-all if she'd just, well, I don't know. Love him, I guess."

"What did she say?"

Jonas looked away towards his own farm. "Nothing," he said. "Nothing that I could hear." He stood up and took a few steps forward. "But after that's when all them hex-signs of yours got going."

"Then you know what they mean?"

Jonas looked at him. "I don't know nothing except they was

some kind of a joke between your mama and daddy and that it tickled them something powerful."

He began to pace, and an angry note entered his voice. "Well, every time the weather was right and all, daddy'd be back up there a-making more of that corn-whiskey of his, drinking it more then he should've and a-taking it out on Ma sometimes. But I knowed what he was a-hoping." Jonas's glance struck out from under his heavy brows towards Matteo. "Well, one night I was a-waiting and it happened again. He was half bawling his eyes out down there and she didn't say nothing. Then all at once something come down out of the trees and he ducked like it hit him on the head. Then he just picked it up and went on home."

Jonas made to walk away himself, and Matteo stood up, calling after him. "What was it?"

Jonas put his hand into his pocket, pulled out something and threw it to Matteo. Matteo looked down at his feet, and in the growing moonlight he saw the spinning top he had given to Marcus. He picked it up, turned it over and saw that it was not the same one after all — the one he held was slightly smaller and a great deal older. Around its four sides someone had painted the letters P A T N. Matteo turned it on his open palm for a moment.

"What does it mean?" Matteo looked up to see that Jonas had disappeared. *"What does it mean?"* he shouted.

There was silence before Jonas's voice came out of the cedar brake that screened the fallen tree. "It's a game. Just an old game."

Matteo went in the direction of the voice, but when he came through the trees he saw no one.

"A game," Matteo repeated distractedly.

"Something most folks 'round here could play." Jonas was sitting amid the rubbish and timber that Matteo had re-piled.

"How do you play?"

"It's called 'Put-and-Take.' Ya can play it for anything ya like: pennies, peanuts, or pigs' tails. It was how Daddy come to have that still in the first place when your granddaddy up and lost it to him a-playing it."

Matteo remembered what Ephraim had said to him about his own grandfather's boast.

"All ya got to do is spin the top," Jonas said. "If you're playing for little things and it comes up P then ya got to put in something. If it comes up T, you can take out something."

Matteo looked at the top. "What about A?"

Jonas was silent for a moment, then he cleared his throat and spoke up. "That's all—everything— all ya want and all there is."

"And N?"

Jonas stood up and looked down the hillside towards his farm, to where the lights shone in the windows. "That's nothing. Just nothing. Means ya lose it all."

Matteo sat down on the log, his back to the older man.

After a while, Jonas spoke again, still not looking at Matteo, but staring out now towards the dim waves of the mountainside opposite. "Daddy must've took it serious, but I never knew whether he got all or nothing. He kept on a-watching the woods, then one night he heard them again. This time he waited and waited, but they didn't never seem to be a-getting done. I was a-laying just down there, just down there," and Jonas pointed into the darkness, "when I heard something go down in the leaves." Jonas swallowed hard. "It must've been an animal or … or … Daddy a-tripping over one of them wires they had strung 'round."

Matteo looked at Jonas, and his neighbour's eyes were wide as he recalled the scene.

"Then," Jonas said, "faster than lightning there was a shot, and a … and a … somebody fell down out of that tree. Then out of somewheres, she screamed. God-a-mercy she screamed … and right then I knowed they had changed places that night in the tree just to make a fool out of Daddy. Just to make a fool out of him."

In the deep shadows drawn by the starlight, Matteo saw Jonas's shoulders heaving as he started to sob. "It was the last time I saw Daddy alive," he muttered as he sat down on the rotting tree. "He disappeared for a week, and then … he was all black and green and the buzzards had…"

Matteo could hear nothing but the breeze and the choking sounds Jonas made. He waited. He knew there was more.

"He had up and hung his self in the … in this God-damn LAR tree." Jonas stopped, unable to speak anymore.

Through the ringing in his ears, Matteo heard the faint echo of his parents' laughter, as they had laughed so often in his boyhood. Their love for one another had blinded them to the folly of making a joke out of another's desire. Crazed by ridicule, one man had killed another in order to make the laughter stop. His parents' passion had led to his father's death, and to his mother's growing old in loneliness.

Matteo stood up. "You lied to me," he said. "You told me you knew nothing. You wanted me to believe the story about the poisoned water. You're a liar and a coward. And you betrayed me."

Jonas's eyes seemed to be looking straight through Matteo, through the forest behind him, through to the hills behind the forest, and beyond to the long endless years of pain and fear.

Matteo bent down to pick up the axe from where it lay at his feet. Just as his fingers touched it, he felt Jonas throw himself against his body.

As the two of them spun around, Matteo saw an explosion of blue-white fire before a spatter of blood sprayed over his face and eyes.

The long thin comb of a wave ran noiselessly over a vacant stretch of the Tyrrhenian Sea before rattling to its climax in the pebbles at Matteo's feet.

He stood with his back to the green-and-blue flecked mountains of the *mezzogiorno* and looked out far to the west as the light of another dawn ran before him into the distances.

The night before he had dreamt again the dream of blue-white light that often troubled his sleep since his return. In the stinging fire of that shotgun blast, he heard and saw over and over again the despair of love made sick with wanting.

It was Esther who had brought the gun along with her up the high and lonely hillside. Frightened and confused by what she saw, she took aim at nothing so much as the struggle that embraced them all. A single piece of shot ricocheted directly through one of Jonas's cheeks and out the other side, just as his face had drawn close to Matteo's.

Writhing and spitting blood, Jonas tore the shotgun from her hands. The three of them stood stock-still in the sudden weird silence until a glimmer of moonlight revealed the seriousness of Jonas's wound.

As Matteo looked into Jonas's fierce and beaten eyes, he heard him struggle out a few halting words.

"It was her," he said, "her and me that cut it down. Lar — your mama — and me. We cut it down. 'Till the saw broke."

Then Jonas released him, and Matteo had fallen backwards, half onto the ground, half-propped against a tree. His arms lay outwards on either side, stretched in a futile gesture, resting on the stones on either side of him.

He lay there dumbly, watching the first arching streaks of the dawn come in bands of turquoise and blue over the horizon.

The sun itself never seemed to rise, but a mistiness settled in, gradually turning to rain. For hours he stayed without moving, empty of illusion, devoid of dreams. At last, the dryness of his mouth burnt into him, and he cried out in his loneliness and despair, too empty even to bring tears.

In the long shadow of afternoon, while the rain in the trees kept up a low and murmuring chant, he finally pulled himself to his feet and walked home.

He stayed indoors for two entire days, cleaning the house, locking away his past and preparing his mind for a different future.

When all was set in order, he went outside again into the sunshine. It was Sunday, and an impenetrable silence hung over the landscape. He put his key once more into the lock and turned, but this time the lock refused to move. He put the key back where he had found it.

Lifting his pack to his back, he saw in the corner of his eye how the rooms inside looked from outside: neat, uncluttered, asleep in time.

In the room where he had worked, the toys sat on their shelves. He had taken nothing with him that he had made himself, leaving behind much more than he had found—a harvest he would never share.

As he walked over the low-water bridge, the only person to see him go was Ruth Ann—late for church, as usual.

She ran a few steps towards Matteo—as if to catch up to him—then stopped, as though she had suddenly realised that she never really could.

Two weeks later, as Matteo looked out the window of the train carrying him south from Rome, he realised that he had tasted none of the food he had planted himself, but instead had left the whole of his parents' garden to run wild once more.

At his destination, he turned his eyes to the place where the mountains ran straight down into the sea and he watched as a bird dived into the water before soaring up again with a fish in its bill.

When there was no one about to listen, he closed his eyes and sang,

Si ch'io mi credo omai che monti e piagge
E fiumi e selve sappian di che tempre
Sia la mia vita, ch'e celata altrui.

When he opened his eyes, the music faded away and there was no sound except his own footsteps and the echoing of a forest beyond the sea.

J.D. Ballam was born in the Appalachian Mountains of western Maryland. The early years of his life there form the basis of his popular memoir, *The Road to Harmony* (1999), which Dirk Bogarde described as "a book to cherish." He is the author of poetry, plays and numerous academic works. He teaches English and Creative Writing at the University of Oxford. He is married with three children.